Eric and Thickpea

Eric and Thickpea

Jill Martin

iUniverse, Inc.
New York Lincoln Shanghai

Eric and Thickpea

iUniverse books may be ordered through booksellers or by contacting:

iUniverse
2021 Pine Lake Road, Suite 100
Lincoln, NE 68512
www.iuniverse.com
1-800-Authors (1-800-288-4677)

Because of the dynamic nature of the Internet, any Web addresses or links contained in this book may have changed since publication and may no longer be valid.

This is a work of fiction. All of the characters, names, incidents, organizations, and dialogue in this novel are either the products of the author's imagination or are used fictitiously.

Illustrations and cover design by Laura Martin

ISBN: 978-0-595-46620-7 (pbk)
ISBN: 978-0-595-90915-5 (ebk)

Printed in the United States of America

Prologue

"You are the most useless piece of flesh I have ever met, boy. Goodness only knows why I even bother with you. I suppose I'll have to deal with this myself."

The short, dumpy woman spoke with a sneer in her voice, causing her companion to flinch. He ran his fingers through his blond hair and let out a strangled laugh.

"Of course not, Gran," he said, his features echoing her sharp nose and pointed chin, his eyes pale and watery. He seemed scared of this bossy woman, as if he could not look her in the face. This was no soft, cuddly grandmother with white hair and knitting needles. Or rather, the features were there, but the white hair was severely wrapped up in a bun, and the knitting needles were brandished like weapons rather than woolly jumper makers. "I am quite capable of sorting it out. I just need a bit more time, that's all."

"Time, my dear, is the one thing we do not have," replied his grandmother harshly. She rose from the kitchen chair that creaked as her weight lifted, and walked to the window. She seemed to be peering through the net curtains at something, or someone, at the front of the house. "I have cast the line in the water, and the girl has taken the bait. She has acted more quickly than I expected, I admit, so we have to move fast. Is your aunt ready?"

"Oh yes, Gran, as usual," the man grunted. His brainy Auntie Audrey always managed to make the rest of the family look stupid. "I didn't need her help, you know that. I just need to get the transport sorted, and we'll be set."

"Then what are you waiting for?" his grandmother snapped as she turned and glared at him. He had always been a disappointment to her, with his ham-fisted clumsiness, when compared to Audrey's orderly existence or the prim neatness of his own father. He stared up at the old woman for a moment, then left the room without another sound, his legs and arms swinging wildly as if he didn't know what to do with them.

She turned back to the window, just in time to see him vanish down the street. A young boy was walking past the gate, pausing to tie a shoelace outside the house as her grandson ambled out into the street. The new arrival seemed to be watching him as he went, following his progress out of the corner of his eye—or was she imagining it? The woman shook her head vigorously. She must be dreaming—she was beginning to see problems where there were none. The sooner this business was completed, the better. Then they could all get on with living a richer, more comfortable life.

1

Dumpster diving

Seven Days to Christmas

A bitterly cold wind howled under the arches of the bridge, whistling through any gaps it could find, and lifting litter and leaves into the air for a crazy dance before hurling them against the brick walls and letting them drop into untidy heaps. The sky was a dark, dirty grey, with wisps of even darker grey scudding past as if in a hurry to be somewhere else. Beneath one of the heaps of wind-blown rubbish, Eric shivered, his eyes wide with cold, the only protection from the biting wind being an old blanket wrapped over his knees and tucked under his chin, and a woolly hat pulled down over his ears. His face was in need of a good wash, and judging by the rumbling noises coming from the depths of his stomach, he was very hungry.

But Eric was used to it. He had lived like this for the past four years. A boy of the underworld was what he called himself, scraping a sort of life on the street, out of sight and mind, uncluttered and unimportant. Big City Life was something that happened to other people, those who lived in houses, owned cars and travelled on the tube trains with a mobile phone glued to an ear, those who spent long hours in squeaky clean offices making more money for those who already have too much, then went to restaurants for big meals, with more well-off, well-dressed, beautiful people. Life just wasn't fair.

Eric reached under his blanket and felt the small furry bundle that snoozed gently. The body shifted slightly with every breath and did not stir at Eric's touch. It was much too cosy in there, definitely not getting-up-time yet, so Eric very carefully tried to stretch out each leg and arm so as not to disturb his companion. Muscle by muscle his limbs straightened, having been curled tightly in the blanket for hours as he slept, and each finger cracked slightly as he moved his hands and willed them to be warm. That was a knack he had learned from Old Yar, the grizzled, ancient sailor from his days spent sailing the freezing waters of the Atlantic many years before. He had taken Eric aside one dark, cold night as they huddled in a shop doorway, leaned close and passed on this small but important piece of help to the boy.

"Whenever you are cold," he muttered under his breath, making Eric think he was being told an amazing secret, "you think hard about being warm. Feel it slowly creep into your hands and feet. Don't try to rush it, just let it happen like it's sneaking up on you. After a while, if you keep at it, your fingers and toes will start to tingle, and gradually get warm. You try it, boy, it's no fantasy."

And sure enough, Old Yar was right. Eric had become quite good at thinking himself warm, particularly when it was the middle of the night and there was only his little furry friend for company. He would lie as still as he could, blocking out all sounds that might disturb his concentration, and thought warm thoughts. Pictures passed through his mind of log fires, cups of hot chocolate, and a comfy sofa to curl up on. A pleasant sensation of calm and peace always overtook him, and the warmth, when it came, always brought a smile to his face. Goodness only knows what anybody would have thought of him if they had seen him lying there, grinning to himself and silently thanking Old Yar for the umpteenth time for telling him the trick. The ancient mariner had a knack of coming up with solutions to little problems that he had had to solve for himself whenever he was miles out to sea.

Eric felt a warm glow creeping into his toes and fingers just as his companion decided to make an entrance. A nose poked out of the pocket and sniffed.

"Oh, at last," whispered Eric, "decided to join the world again, have you?"

The creature looked up into his face, and squeaked. Eric chuckled and reached into his shoulder bag to see if he could find a crumb of food. There wasn't much, so very carefully he lifted the furry little bundle into his hand and put her straight into the bag to rootle around for herself. There must have been enough to keep her going for a while, and eventually she came out cleaning her whiskers.

"Good," said Eric, standing up and stretching his legs fully at last. "Now it's my turn for breakfast."

It was still early, and the sun had not bothered to get up. Thick, dark clouds filled the sky from one end to the other, each one chasing the next out of the way as they headed to somewhere better. Above him Eric heard the cars and buses trundling angrily along as the city started another day, and close by, huge lorries were turning into the superstore car park to unload their goods, their exhausts kicking out a haze of fumes into the chilly morning. Eric licked his lips. The boy's mouth was watering at the thought of those exotic foods coming from all points of the world and ending up on the shelves of the store, ready to be bought by other people, so close by yet out of reach for him. His tummy grumbled. It was definitely time for breakfast.

He was already dressed. The scruffy trainers were a bit tight but still kept most of the weather off his feet. His trousers, thrown out with the rubbish and left behind a bungalow near London Fields station, were so long, he had to roll them up three times. Over the top of a holey jumper and a few t-shirts, Eric wore a grubby mud-coloured jacket that may not have been the colour of mud when it was made. Washing clothes was not a priority when living on the streets.

Eric carefully pushed any sign of his bedroom out of sight in the undergrowth, squashing the dirty blanket into an untidy heap so it would not attract any vagrant thieves, and messing up a pile of dead leaves to hide his other precious things. He picked his way through thorny bushes to a broken fence that led to a bridge over the rail tracks. Then he stood still, looking around, making sure he was quite invisible to the people on their way somewhere. A lady with high heels click-clacked by, holding a phone to her ear and staring at the ground. Two men in suits talked quietly to each other, using their umbrellas for walking sticks as they marched swiftly past. A group of teenage girls, all wearing the same blue and gold uniform, giggled and gossiped merrily on their way to school. Yes, it was just as he had expected—nobody even glanced in Eric's direction. Good.

The search for breakfast took him over the bridge and into the superstore car park, which was home to several large wheelie bins, always a promising place to search for a snack. There were a few cars in the car park already, even though the store had not yet opened, but more worryingly, Eric could hear a low, distinctive rumble drawing near. It must be dustbin-emptying day. He dived his arm into the first bin and rummaged frantically through for any scraps he could reach as the dustbin cart lumbered into the car park. His search became more urgent. Dustbin men did not wait for scavengers. He grabbed the first things he could reach and legged it before the approaching lorry got too close.

Stopping to catch his breath, he saw that his dumpster diving—where had he heard that? Must be an American phrase—had gained him a pack of egg and cress sandwiches, out of date, a plastic cup with half a portion of noodles in some kind of sauce (he hoped it was sweet and sour, which was his favourite), and a bottle of fizzy pop, nearly full (probably packed with additives, but then you have to take what you can get). Not bad for a first trawl of the day, he thought, gathering up his findings and heading out of the car park towards the line of small shops along the main road. Eric reached a row of little shops and cowered in a doorway of a tanning studio. The knack of staying invisible that he had perfected during his years on the streets worked. The waste lorry rumbled out of the superstore car park and down the road past the shops, and the binmen never even glanced in his direction. He settled down to eat his tiny banquet.

2

Soup Buddies

From an early age Eric found it easy to make friends with animals. Whenever the boy heard a telltale rustle or squeak he would freeze, not moving a muscle, allowing whatever it was to come and investigate him and decide that not only was he harmless but also friendly. This was how he ended up having close encounters with many creatures that shared his habitat—grey squirrels, foxes, stray cats and dogs, even a badger once—but his favourites were always the long, sleek rats that dwelled in the tunnels used by the trains. He knew how people hated rats. Even the other vagrants screamed and yelled in fear when they saw one, but Eric found them to be clever, affectionate and loyal—and surprisingly clean.

He knew it was common practice for people to have pets. His informer was Old Yar, who would sit and talk to Eric for hours, relating stories of his life on the high seas. The old sea-captain had roamed the seas with a rich assortment of animal companions, including a cockatiel with a flamboyant yellow comb of feathers on his head, and red cheeks, as if it was always embarrassed; then there was a chameleon, a strange lizard-like creature that moved in slow motion and had odd eyes that thought for themselves. The sailor even claimed to have trained a lion cub, capturing it on a trading voyage to Africa and keeping it on board his ship to deter pirates and stop the crew from even considering mutiny. Eric loved the idea of such a companion, but knew he would never find anything quite so exotic—so a rat would do nicely.

Every spring, as the weather warmed and the smell from the dustbins behind the tightly-packed houses started to hum, he would take a discarded cardboard box from the back of the superstore, put inside it a scrap of meat taken from a wheelie bin, and place it close, but not too close, to the mouth of the railway tunnel near to Stoke Newington station which he knew to be an excellent place to lure the most handsome rats. Once the trap was set, Eric hid behind a pillar, within reach of the bait but out of view of any passing trains and also fairly well sheltered from any rain or cold, and waited.

Patience was not a problem to Eric. He could stay perfectly still for long periods when he needed to—just being invisible, or thinking himself warm, or watching for a safe moment to dash out and grab food from a bin, or waiting until some wild creature felt safe enough to approach him. Then, after what was often quite a long time, rats would appear. Slowly at first they made their way out of the tunnel, noses twitching constantly, on the alert for danger as well as for food. The older, more experienced rats came first, followed by the younger, more reckless ones, which ventured a bit further out than their elders. This was why Eric had positioned his trap not too close to the tunnel mouth.

Sure enough, sooner or later, a young rat would raise its long, twitching nose and catch a whiff of Eric's bait. Then, carefully, step-by-step it came nearer, until the enticing smell took over and it made for the box. Eric had to move quietly now; if the rat realised he was there, then it would be gone before he could lift a leg. So he edged an arm out, reaching over the box, then with a sudden movement he pushed his hand down onto the top of the box, trapping the rat inside. A few scurrying moments later, the rat would go quiet, and then Eric had to carefully scoop up both box and new pet into the folds of his blanket and begin his long walk home.

Then would begin the fun, befriending and training his new pet so that it responded to his voice, fed from his hand, and maybe even came when he called. He usually ended up scarred and bloody during the early training sessions, but in the end he gained the trust and affection of his new friend as it realised he was not a threat, was a great source of regular food, and offered a comfy place to sleep.

By catching a fresh rat every year, Eric could make sure his pet was always young and healthy, and no matter what, the creature was always set free the following year. Eric had seen dogs kept in cages, or tied to long chains, behind the tightly packed houses, and thought it was cruel, as every animal deserves freedom at some time in its life.

Then came the task of choosing names for his pets. After some deliberation Eric latched on to one happy memory in his vagrant life—the times in the depths of winter when the Big City celebrated Christmas, and he and the other vagrants went to stay in a hostel for a while, with new and familiar faces for company, a hot bath, a comfortable bed, and plenty of warming, comforting food. He chose to call his rats after the hot, tasty soups he remembered having during these visits.

His first rat was called Lentil, a beast with a distinctly red tinge to its fur, setting it apart from the usual brown ones. Lentil loved to travel in Eric's shoulder bag, his head and front paws sticking out as he watched everything go by, whiskers twitching as if interested but unwilling to leave the safety of his home. This eagerness to eavesdrop on life meant he was seen by strangers, which caused a bit of a stir each time. Eric had got used to the screaming females, and even managed to fight off one angry old man who tried to yank Lentil out of his bag; but he considered himself to be the carer of his pets, having taken them from their natural life and inflicted these indignities on them, so he fought back whenever they were threatened by unenlightened folk. It had been hard for Eric to let Lentil go as he was so affectionate, but he did in the end, as a promise is a promise, even if it did mean shedding a few unmanly tears in the process.

Mulligatawny, Eric's next rat, could never stand being near any person who was smoking a cigarette. If anybody walked by with a fag hanging from his lips, the rat would snarl, leap out of Eric's bag, jump over whatever distance lay between, scamper up the person's front, grab the cigarette out of his or her mouth, and spit it out onto the pavement. He would then leap back to Eric, vanishing into the folds of his bag, before the astonished stranger even realized what had happened. The first time Eric witnessed it, he could only stand and stare at the victim, whose cigarette-less mouth was wide open with surprise, bereft of speech. For a while after that he tried crossing the street whenever a smoker went by so that he or she was not accosted by Mulligatawny, but it did not work—he simply ran further to reach his quarry, on one occasion nearly being knocked down by a passing car. This must have scared Eric, so much so that he made a point of moving closer to the target, trying to make any leap less dangerous for the rat and also less obvious in the process, and as Mulligatawny returned to hide in his pocket nest he proceeded to walk on as if nothing had happened, leaving the smoker—or ex-smoker—standing alone in the street, speechless and bewildered!

Then there was Scotch Broth. He had a short tail, possibly having lost it in a fight as a youngster, but it didn't stop him being a cheeky little creature. Scotch Broth's favourite prank was to run up Eric's back inside his jumper, then scuttle down his sleeve, lick Eric's fingers, then dash back up the sleeve, heading for the other arm, tickling him as he went and making him chuckle aloud—a rare sound for the lad to make. Scotch Broth travelled far and wide after he was let back into the wild, and it was through his tales to other rats that the stream of potential partners for Eric made their way to Stoke Newington every spring.

After Scotch Broth came Leek, so named because he wee'd as soon as he saw Eric for the first time! Pale eyes set him apart from the others—eyes that darted nervously from side to side all the time. Eric decided he must have been an extremely ineffective guard dog in a previous life, and indeed he did not last long in this life. Eric paid a visit to Old Yar's shelter one warm autumn evening, to 'yarn', as the old sailor called it, along with Doldrum, a woman with the most wonderful chocolate-coloured skin and an infectious smile, and Whiskers, an old vagrant with a glass eye. Doldrum had told him Whiskers got his name because he was completely bald, just as she was called Doldrum because she was always jolly and finding something to laugh about. That evening Eric ambled to the old deserted school near Hackney Downs, Leek keeping a look-out from his shoulder bag until Eric reached the pile of rags that made up Old Yar's bed, then leapt up onto the sailor's lap in welcome. It was a fatal move. Eric had not realised his white-haired friend had a new pet of his own, a fine-looking cream-coloured ferret called Binnacle that defended its territory with ferocity. Eric left alone after their yarn, his cheeks wet, a little sadder but also a lot wiser.

Which brings us to the latest rat, named after Eric's favourite soup of the moment, Thickpea. It did not seem a silly name to the boy, no more daft than calling a dog Bonzo, or a cat Fifi, and meant much more, because it always reminded him of happy times spent with the other homeless. Over the months that Eric had cared for Thickpea, he became aware of the creature's intelligence and sensitivity, and so were drawn very close together. She was the first female rat he had caught, and somehow Eric knew he was going to have second thoughts about letting her go in the spring.

Thickpea's colouring wasn't exceptional. She had a brown coat, long, thin, whippy tail, whiskers that loved to twitch and tiny black eyes that stuck out from the side of her head, giving a clear view behind as well as in front. All rats are clever, able to fend for themselves and work out the best way to get what they want, but not enough to solve a problem, read a mind, or communicate. Well, this particular rat had a brain that she knew how to use, and a strange gift that Winnie the bag-lady called 'feeling awareness'. It was a quality that helped Eric more than he could have guessed over the following days.

Over the months, as boy and rat became closer and more in tune with each other, Eric learned that this was not Thickpea's only special quality. She could feel the emotions of those close by. It made her a useful ally, able to detect danger and warn her beloved Eric. Some people may have considered it a curse, feeling what people are thinking simply by the way they look at Eric, but it was a talent that would later save Eric's life. A look of hatred gave her a flush of cold, starting at the tail and working up to the ears, whereas annoyance made the ears twitch. A soft glow of warmth made the rat shudder gently, and sadness was shown by a strange, unearthly squeal that seemed to rip through Eric's ears and into the huge empty cavern that was his head. Not a pleasant sensation—but an easy one to interpret.

It did not take long for Thickpea to understand what Eric said to her. She learned to read Eric's moods, staying hidden when he was angry, coming closer and nuzzling his nose when he was upset or feeling particularly lonely, and even frolicking beside him on the rare occasions when he ran, pranced, sang and laughed along the embankment in the warm sun. Sometimes, as they snuggled close at night, with Eric wrapped in his grubby blanket and the rat tunnelling up and down the sleeves of his jumper, they would play a game, with Eric rubbing a scrap of food in his fingers, then hiding it somewhere for Thickpea to find. She would sniff Eric's fingers, then stand for a moment, whiskers twitching as she got the scent, then put her nose down and trail her way to the morsel. She won the game every time, but Eric didn't mind. It felt calm and soothing to see his little companion chomping away, almost silently, eyes half closed with happiness, then wiping her whiskers with her paws as she looked up at Eric, squeaked a thank-you, and buried herself back in her pocket nest. Then Eric would settle for the night, resting his head on his shoulder bag and letting his mind go blank as sleep wrapped them both up and kept them safe until morning.

3

The Hat Girl

It came as quite a surprise to Eric that Thickpea was remarkably choosy about her food. Rats have a reputation for eating anything and everything that falls in their path, but in reality they are far more likely to select a tender piece of rare steak than a trodden-on hot dog. That morning, as they ate their breakfast, the rat sniffed warily at the morsel of cold noodle she had been offered, then turned her head away with a look of disgust before nosing the sandwich packet as a hint. A bit of egg with a sprinkling of cress was more to her liking, and the hint worked.

A tin can rattled along the pavement and a chorus of shouts and laughter heralded the arrival of a gang of boys, kicking the can to each other in a game of mock football. They tackled and weaved with their can as they passed, concentrating so hard on their game that they paid no heed to Eric, who shrank further into the shadows of the tanning shop doorway as soon as he heard their approach. He knew these boys. He had seen them many times before. One of the gang, a tall, lanky individual with hair hidden beneath a hat pulled over his ears, yelled orders to his cronies as he controlled their progress past the shops. His face was round and pale, with a nose that had been broken at some time and a thin, wide mouth; but most striking were his eyes. They seemed far too big for his face, and were—well, it was hard to tell their colour without close staring, but they were so pale as to be almost colourless. This was Kal, leader of the gang that called itself the Fractured Jawbones. Eric had been lucky enough never to have encountered Kal and his mates personally. He intended to keep it that way. The boys continued their game until they went out of sight round the corner, heading away from the shops and back towards the superstore, no doubt making for the car park where they could use the wheelie bins as goal posts, or create a bit of graffiti art on the superstore walls. Eric had watched over the past months as the gang had perfected their graffiti style. At first their sign had been 'Jawbones', written in multicoloured cans of spray paint, but that had soon been shortened to 'Jawz'. That distinctive tag now graced the sides of most of the shops and offices in the Seven Sisters area of London, and caused a great deal of annoyance among the local businesses. In the silence that followed the disappearance of Kal and his mates into the superstore car park Eric and Thickpea finished munching their breakfast.

With the worst of the stomach pangs gone, Eric popped Thickpea back into his pocket and wandered past the rest of the shops. The idea had been to scavenge the other bins to find more food for later, but now they had been emptied, they were forced to look elsewhere for their next meal. The rat snuggled down in the top pocket of Eric's brown wool jacket speckled with creamy white, and passed the time picking at the seam, making the hole she was excavating larger and better for sneaking a glimpse of the world and listening to conversations.

Their wanderings took them down Florin Avenue, a wide road with two ranks of large brick houses; then into Tanner Lane, with its narrower roadway, then along Farthing Road, also tightly packed with vehicles. These were streets they knew from their daily treks, as Eric made his way from one haven to the next. He had established three hideouts, each one stocked with essentials for a comfortable existence—an old blanket, a piece of plastic sheeting for when it rained, a pile of stone-free earth for a bed and a tin box with just a handful of treasured possessions. It was safer to keep these spread between the three havens, just in case one were found and raided by children at play or some other underworlder looking to increase his own stock of precious items. Thickpea's favourite haven was the one they had left that morning, under the railway bridge close to the shops at Seven Sisters, and near the superstore with its supply of bins and rubbish always available for her to explore. She had enjoyed many adventures by herself foraging there already. The next nearest haven was in the cemetery near Stoke Newington railway station, where a quiet corner was shielded by long grass, an overgrown yew tree and an ancient obelisk. Eric had man-handled an abandoned gravestone to make a slanting roof, forming a spot where the weather could only penetrate on very blustery days. This was the most peaceful of Eric's havens, as not many people visited the graves nearby and the caretaker was contented to leave that patch wild. The third haven, in a neglected back garden near the green at Hackney Downs, was not used much, so Eric thought of it as an emergency bolthole. There was also the old school near Hackney Downs railway sta-tion, where Old Yar and Winnie the bag-lady liked to spend their time and where he was assured of company and some comfort.

Farthing Road lay closer to Stamford Hill Station than Seven Sisters. It was lined with old brick-fronted houses, each one with a well-tended front garden. Cars were parked outside the painted front doors, some fresh and clean, others rather shabby and peeling. Eric always tried to see into the windows as he passed, wondering what the occupants were doing at that moment. That wasn't hard to imagine that morning; it was still early, and most house dwellers would still be tucked up in their warm, soft beds. Eric remembered beds. He had been given one at the Christmas hostel, and after so many months sleeping in the open it had taken him several nights to get used to it. By the time he was used to the comfort and relaxed enough to get a good night's sleep, he had to leave and head back to his vagrant life.

Sure enough, most of the windows on Farthing Road wore curtains tightly pulled across, keeping the insides hidden from view. Eric turned his attention to the gardens, most of which were rather bare, with squares of lawn edged with brown earth and a few pots with colourful cabbage-like plants growing next to the front door. All very neat, he thought. In the front garden of number seven, however, was an unexpected pile of rubbish. A heap of old clothes had been left in a corner, close to the wall. Dear me, he wondered, what is the neighbourhood coming to? Then, as he walked on, the heap sneezed.

Eric looked back to see the clothing shake as a small figure appeared from its hibernation, rubbing sleep from its eyes and yawning widely.

"Hello, Bonnet," Eric said softly.

The figure turned to face him. At first terror showed in the wide, black eyes before dissolving into a scowl. Thickpea twitched, feeling her gaze as a quick, sharp dig in the ribs that faded to a dull ache as Bonnet became calmer.

"Oh, it's you," she muttered, slowly stretching her arms over her head and letting her heap of bedding cascade to the ground. "Well, just keep it down, there's a good chap. I'm on surveillance, and you might blow my cover."

Eric was used to Bonnet's unusual ways of speaking. He looked closely at her, and saw she had an old tatty Sherlock Holmes-type deerstalker hat on her head. Bonnet was about fifteen years old, and was quite plain—slim and leggy, elegant in her movements, her long dark hair hung limply around her oval face, but her eyes were remarkable. Deep pools of black that could shine with emotion were watching Eric with an annoyed glare. He lifted his foot onto the low stone wall, trying to look as if he was nonchalantly tying a shoelace.

"What is it this time?"

Bonnet looked furtively up and down the street.

"A disappearance. A child has gone missing, and I saw a suspicious-looking rogue entering that house over there, number four. I'm waiting for him to come out again."

"A missing child? Oh yes, I remember, I saw it on the newspaper board this morning. And what are this rogue's distinguishing features, then?" Eric knew how to talk to her when she was in detective mode.

"Short, blond hair, a nose long enough to probe a termite's nest, and very pale, watery eyes. I think he must have been an anteater in a previous life—though he must have been a weedy one. He'll never be a basketball player, much too short, no muscle in his upper legs. He has eggs for breakfast most days, judging by the mess on his t-shirt. He doesn't smile much, and the downward turn of his mouth suggests a grumpy nature. Other than that, I wouldn't recognise him at all. Look out—"

She ducked back into her heap of clothes as the front door on Number 4 opened and a skinny youngish man with short blond hair came out and waddled along the pavement in the direction of the shops. Eric, still trying to tie his shoelace, watched him out of the corner of his eye as he vanished round the corner into Tanner Lane. He looked vaguely familiar—but he couldn't work out why.

The deerstalker hat rose out of the rubbish heap, and Bonnet's face followed.

"I say, old thing, would you do me a favour?" Her eyes softened as she turned her gaze to Eric. "Just follow him for me, see where he goes, then pop back and fill me in. Unless you've got another appointment. If you're not too busy—mmm?"

Eric smiled.

"Well, I was on my way to do some business for Winnie, but I suppose it can wait."

Bonnet beamed at him.

"Good man! I'll see you right, don't you worry. Now off you go, or you'll lose him. Chop chop!"

He finished tying his lace with a flourish, and moved off, careful to look away from Bonnet's hiding place. The young man had long since vanished from view, and he had to walk quickly to make up for lost time. Thickpea shuffled a little in her pocket as he set off.

Bonnet was quite a character, even amongst the wealth of rich personalities Eric had met. She had an amazing talent, quite unlike anything Eric had seen before. She always carried a bag full to the brim with hats, each one different, and she wore whichever suited the occasion. She would wear a broad-rimmed straw sunhat for hot afternoons in the park, a flat cap when she wanted to blend in with the crowds at a football match, an army helmet for dangerous days, and a balaclava when she robbed banks. There was a game hunter's pith helmet to use when stalking prey, and she could chat to little old ladies on the park bench in her felt hat adorned with cherries. Eric never worked out how she could carry so many hats in just one bag. But more amazing still was the fact that as soon as Bonnet put on any hat, she would change her personality to match. Her posture would change, her voice and language took on the right tone and grammar, and she could be the very person who would wear that hat in normal life. She was like a chameleon, changing herself to any occasion, simply by putting on a different hat. The other vagrants found her a bit spooky, but Eric loved the fact that he never knew who she was going to be whenever he saw her.

"Well, Thickpea," he whispered as he walked on, "we'd better keep an eye out for headlines. There's bound to be news of another mystery solved by Sherlock Bonnet very soon." The rat squeaked in reply and snuggled deeper into her pocket nest.

Eric was a good choice of person to trail a suspect, as he was particularly good at being invisible. He felt most at home when he was not in view, keeping himself hidden from the gaze of the people who walked the streets with a purpose, striding purposefully on their way. Eric did not like attracting attention when in public. In fact, when the stares of passers-by became very intense, such as when he wandered through a crowd of commuters making their determined way to the station to work while he was dressed in his scruffy jacket and jeans and in need of a good wash, the attention even made him feel sick. It was not a feeling he was proud of, so he tried to avoid any situation that might bring it about.

Eric turned the next corner, back into Tanner Lane and heading towards the railway again. There was the man, his waddling walk making him easy to spot as more and more people were heading out of their houses and making their way to the station. He turned left down a narrow path between two houses, and Eric had to speed up to keep him in view. As he reached the end of the alleyway, he saw Blondie, as he decided to call him, vanish through a gate on the right side of the track which led into one of the back yards that lined the path.

Eric waited for a short while to make sure the man had gone into the house and would not see him; then he walked stealthily forward to make sure he would remember which back yard it was. Number 27, Pickering Avenue. Thickpea squeaked three times gently in her pocket hiding place. Eric could have sworn she had said 'Twenty-seven' in rat language. Then he turned and sped back to Bonnet to pass on his information.

As they approached 7 Farthing Road, a dirty white van sped round the corner, its tyres squealing as it nearly turned on its side in the haste of its departure. Eric stopped and watched it zoom off. He'd heard of White Van Man as a breed of bad driver; was there such a thing, much worse than that, called Dirty White Van Man? Well, there was now.

The heap of old clothes was still there in the front garden of 7 Farthing Road, as if it had been tipped out of a charity bag and left abandoned under the window; but there was no movement, no sign of life. Bonnet's beloved bag of hats, her most treasured possession, the one thing she would never leave behind, had been tipped out and its contents strewn all over the front garden. There was no sign of the girl herself. Eric felt a cold shudder start in his pocket before it sped through his body. He had picked up Thickpea's sensitive radar. Bonnet was in danger.

4

Breaking and Entering

Things were definitely not right. Eric scanned the debris, searching for a hint of where Bonnet had gone. She never went anywhere without her hat bag; the fact that it remained and she had vanished meant trouble.

"What's going on?" Eric muttered, casting his eye further afield over the whole of the garden. "Perhaps for once in her life she was on to something real, and had been found out. What d'you think, Thickpea?"

Thickpea stuck her head as far as she dared out of the pocket, and sniffed. There was a dull odour of stale tobacco, and a whiff of underarm pong. A man, that much she could discern from the scent, and not a very fastidious one at that. Boy and rat looked at each other in unspoken agreement.

"Better be careful," Eric glanced down the street nervously. "Don't want to get noticed. I can't leave it, though—let's have a look around, okay?"

He made his way along to the next road junction, where Guinea Close joined Farthing Road, and headed to what he hoped would be the rear of number seven. Sure enough, a rough track led down behind the houses, leading to each back garden and its rather dilapidated sheds and garages. The back gardens were hidden behind high wooden fences, so he kept out of view, until he reached the back gate of number seven. It was painted the same dark green as the front door. Eric lifted the latch as carefully as he could, and entered.

There was nobody in sight, but he couldn't be sure of not being spotted. It is all too easy for house dwellers to misjudge the best intentions of vagrants, blaming them for every problem, from outright burglary to pinching of the cream off a bottle of milk. This attitude led Eric to keep in the shadows.

The back door was slightly ajar. Eric made his way towards it, ducking under the kitchen window, then gently pushing the door with the flat of his hand. He stuck his head inside. There was nobody in sight.

"Well, old mate, do we go in, or do we go for help?"

His whispered question made Thickpea jump, she had been so tense.

"You see, we vagrants are not trustworthy. That's the general impression among the house people, so we would be presumed guilty before I had even opened my mouth—and they wouldn't even need to think of what we're guilty of. We need to take a look, though. I tell you what—how about *you* doing it?"

His mind made up, he reached up to lift Thickpea onto his hand, then placed her gently on the ground by the open door. To have anybody put such trust in a mere rat was a great honour, and she determined not to let him down.

Thickpea found herself in a light, airy kitchen, with silver cupboard doors, unblemished work surfaces, and every utensil and appliance in its place. Here lived a very ordered mind, and that meant a person who would not appreciate having his home given the once-over by a rat. She walked through to an open door on the opposite wall, trying to leave no sign of her presence on the spotless floor, and a passing thought occurred to her—she may find some excellent nosh in those cupboards—but she had a mission, and must not fail. There were still no noises to suggest that anybody was coming, so on she went.

The living room was so neat, it looked as though it had never been used. Woe betide anybody who came in there with dirty feet, or dropped crumbs, or even moved too much and made dust. Thickpea knew that house dwellers were house-proud, but this was ridiculous. A sofa stood with its back to the wall, and she crossed behind a matching armchair as she went towards a large desk set in the bay window, with a computer on it set out ready for use. The rat leapt on the chair, which to her surprise swivelled round as she landed, then up onto the desktop to see whether Bonnet's pile of bed was visible from there. It wasn't. But there was a pile of letters, bills and other bits of post that had not been sorted yet, and she thought it was worth a rummage to see what she could find. Even in the few months she had lived with Eric, Thickpea had learned to recognize letters and could put them together to form words, making her more intelligent than some humans, or so Eric had said. The top sheet was an advertisement for a skin cream that reduced the appearance of wrinkles. Then there was another for thermal underwear, to keep out the worst of the winter cold—she nearly took this to show Eric, he would have found it useful. Then an envelope, with handwriting on it and the soft yellow colour of a cool winter sun, addressed to 'Miss A. Butler, 7 Farthing Road'. As she tried to lift these out of the way, it dropped to the floor. A corner of the letter itself fell out, and the rat saw the words '—that street girl—' and '—get her to tell us—'. Her reading was slow, but she understood. That letter was about Bonnet. She felt a shiver run down her spine and knew the letter meant danger, but she took a deep breath, swallowed her fear, grabbed it and its envelope in her mouth, and started to make her way rather slowly now to the back door. Whatever had happened to Bonnet had something to do with this Miss A. Butler and 7 Farthing Road.

A sudden chill rippled through her body, causing her to freeze to the spot. Thickpea's hair stood on end, and a paralysing terror rooted her feet to the floor. Then, from somewhere behind her, came a deep, rumbling murmur. There was a person in the room, somebody she had missed before, and there she was, standing in full view, right in the middle of the carpet.

She turned very slowly, preparing to drop her prize and flee for her life. There, dangling around the side of the armchair, was a hand, chubby fingers empty, the wrist wearing a thin gold chain. Whoever was in that chair was massive, And Thickpea gingerly moved forward to get a better look, still alert to the possibility that she may have to scarper. It was a man, with two fat arms like tree trunks draped off the edges of the chair, his face round and flabby, the mouth open, the eyes tightly closed. He was asleep. At regular intervals a horrible growling snore poured out of his mouth, making his bloated tummy heave up then drop back down as his braces twanged with the strain. His head was bald apart from a few long strands that were dragged across from one ear to the other in an attempt to cover up the shiny pate. A dribble of spit had dropped onto his shirtfront, mingling with cigarette ash and making a kind of concrete slurry that threatened to set solid. His tummy was decorated with a colourful array of food remains; tomato ketchup, chocolate sauce, greasy rubbed patches where a chip had been dropped then picked up and eaten. This was not a hygienic man. Even rats were cleaner than this human! What on earth was such a human dustbin doing in this spotless, gleaming property?

But what shook Thickpea far more than his appearance, even more than the shock of finding him there at all, was the fact that in the depths of her memory, she recognized the slob in front of her! He had played a part in her past, a time she had thought dead and buried, before her life with Eric, when the world had been a darker place. He had done things to her, things she had spent the rest of her life trying to forget. He had caused her pain, and she knew he had killed other rats with his actions. The misery of her younger days flooded back, and for a moment she was desperately lost, the sense of powerless terror overwhelming her as it had many months before.

It took all her self-control and inner strength to pull herself back to the present. Yes, he was the same man—what had they called him? Sprockett, that was it! But he was asleep. He did not know she was there. The thought of escaping from him twice in a lifetime was too good to be true; but with a huge effort Thickpea clenched her teeth, making sure the lemon-yellow letter was still safely in her grasp, then turned and ran as fast as her legs would move to get out of that room and away from that man. She would have time to work out what it all meant later.

Thickpea found the boy where she had left him, waiting under the kitchen window, and ran straight to him, dropping her prize in front of him and nuzzling his hand frantically to soothe herself.

"Well done, kid," Eric murmured, carefully lifting Thickpea, stroking her head gently. He retrieved the lemon-tinted notepaper, examining it as he thrust it into his shoulder bag.

"Miss A Butler. That rings a bell, something from years ago, when I was a kid."

But he said no more. There seemed to be too many things he half recognized that day. He put it down to the strange circumstances playing tricks on his mind.

Then they made their way out of the garden, again making sure they were not observed. Thickpea had nestled down in her pocket, still very shaken by her encounter. Rounding the corner of Farthing Road, they were passed by a young man striding purposefully towards the house they had just left. It was Blondie. Eric shrank back to avoid being seen, but the man seemed to be preoccupied and never even glanced in his direction. They stopped to see him return into the front door of number seven, and only then did Eric continue on his way. He scooped up Bonnet's hats and other belongings as best he could, and hurried away. The least he could do was to put her precious possessions in a safe place until she could reclaim them. Then Eric and Thickpea headed for Hackney Downs.

5

Chinwag

The most important thing about living without a solid roof over your head is keeping your space and your belongings safe. You don't have much, which makes each tiny item very treasured, and a true vagrant will always respect a person's privacy and possessions. This is what Eric had been led to believe by Old Yar, who in his many years on the streets had met his fair share of thieving and dishonest vagrants with no thought for anyone but themselves.

It seemed to make sense to have more than one haven, so that he would never be far from something of his own, and should one stash be found he would not lose everything. The railway bridge near Seven Sisters hid a thick jacket he had been given one winter, along with a toothbrush and a comic. In the Hackney Downs garden was a box containing half a pair of earrings, possibly gold, an old French franc, some safety pins and a fork, all scavenged as he travelled around his patch. At the cemetery near Stoke Newington Eric hid his most valuable items—a small knife in a leather sheath, a pencil, a woolly hat and a pair of gloves, all stuffed down the back of a low wall under a granite gravestone.

His route that morning took him away from the houses, through a field of long grass that the local homeless called the Gypsy Meadow, as that was where the Romany's left their horses tethered whenever they came into the area. Then on over a bridge, under which ran a main road leading into the city, and on until he reached a high fence. He walked round the perimeter to where he knew there was a gap in the wire, and slipped through. It did not have to be a wide gap; Eric was skinny enough to crawl through very thin spaces. Then it was back to civilization, through the streets, along the embankment, round the edge of a football pitch, then over a couple of fences and into the Hackney Downs garden.

Eric had hollowed out a tiny cave in the earth, topped it with dead wood and more soil, then blocked it from view with a large piece of rotting trellis still draped with some sort of climbing plant. It had taken several weeks to complete, as he could only work at night, and had to be quiet for fear of disturbing the large, brown dog next door. Once the haven had been finished, Eric then went about the task of slowly becoming familiar with the dog, so that it eventually accepted him and no longer growled or barked when he arrived. The house that fronted the garden was a terraced dwelling with a long, thin grass lawn edged with shrubs and weeds, and was owned by a young couple who only came out of the back door when they needed to have a cigarette.

Once inside the haven, there was a surprising amount of room, with the low-roofed edges ideal for keeping the few items Eric needed, and in one darker than usual corner he carefully stowed Bonnet's hats. Then without so much as a glance at the house, he retraced his steps to the embankment, and headed along the track.

Hackney Mansions was once a school, but now it was a heap of derelict buildings with leaking roofs and plenty of scope for the likes of Eric and his vagrant friends. Grass grew through the concrete slabs in the old playground, and nearly every one of the dozen big rooms had a large blackboard, where Eric would draw to his heart's content and leave messages for his friends. He loved visiting there, knowing he could have time to himself in one of the many empty rooms, or he could sit with the others who shared his way of life and put the world to rights, while Thickpea sneaked off to be with others of her kind. Thus it was that day, and the rat headed for the darker, damper corners to meet the other furry residents of the Mansions. She never despised the other rats, even though her life was much more pleasant and comfortable than theirs, and she was always welcomed with—well, not exactly open paws, but certainly friendly squeaks rather than bared teeth and claws. They would scamper from room to room for a while, re-acquainting themselves with each other's smells and twitches, then would join together to scavenge for any dropped crumbs or other rubbish in the nearby gardens and dustbins. Not much hope of a feast, but you never know.

Eric followed the long corridor and made for the old school staff room with its handful of mouldy armchairs and coffee tables still littered with chipped mugs and tatty old books. Old Yar the sailor was sprawled on the lowest, widest and softest chair, sunk so deep in the folds of material that it looked as if it was trying to swallow him whole. His mop of white hair was topped with a peaked cap, and a dark, wooden pipe hung from his lips. He had almost forgotten the taste of tobacco, he once told Eric, but he couldn't bear to be without his old pipe. A thick coat was wrapped tightly around his skinny frame, and he toyed with a piece of thick rope as he sat, clearly in the middle of another tale of his seafaring past. Opposite him were two more chairs, where a man and a woman sat, not quite so hidden by the upholstery but still sinking on the soft springs and soggy sponges that made up their seat cushions.

"It's the boy!" Old Yar exclaimed as Eric walked in, and he clambered out of the chair with some difficulty, came forward with a wide-legged stagger typical of a man who had spent years at sea, and shook him warmly by the hand. "We've had too many high tides since we saw you last, my lad. How are you?"

Eric released his hand from the sailor's ironclad grip and smiled at the others.

"I'm okay, thanks," he said, heading for a spot on a rug by the feet of the nearest chair. "And you're all well?"

The woman leaned forward and touched his hair. A pair of plastic bags tied to the old woman's belt rustled as she moved.

"I've been worried about you, Eric," she said, frowning, "it's so not good to have a young lad out there on his own. You need to get yourself a proper base, somewhere we can look out for you. Especially now you're growing up."

Her attempts to include modern speech patterns had become part of her character, and Eric no longer found them unusual or amusing. He rather appreciated the old lady's efforts to join in with the younger people she met.

"Stop mothering the boy, Winnie," Old Yar scolded. "He's old enough and ugly enough to cope by now. Don't worry about her, boy. She's suffering with her—what is it now?"

Winnie wriggled in her chair.

"Asteroids, dear."

Eric hid a smile. Winnie meant haemorrhoids. Old Yar coughed. He shouldn't have asked.

"It's been—how many years now, boy?"

"Four," muttered Eric, staring at his knees. He did not like talking about himself.

Eric found it hard to talk freely with other people. Some folk are tough and selfish, even amongst the other vagrants—stealing from each other and fighting over silly things like a large sheet of cardboard that would make a reasonable blanket on a cold night. The only people Eric spent time with these days were this handful of vagrants he had accepted as friends, who scavenged a living on the city streets as he did, sleeping under bridges, travelling along the railway embankments out of sight of the people on the streets, living off the few scraps they found in the dustbins of the tightly-packed brick houses close to the tracks, but keeping a sort of moral code despite the hardships, refusing to turn to theft or violence. That was one thing Eric wouldn't do; stealing and hurting others was wrong, he had been told—not that he could remember who by. Anyway, it would be just his luck to get caught; so he was too cowardly, or sensible, depending on your point of view, to try it.

His oldest companion, Old Yar, was a tall, broad-chested man with a magnificent chalky white beard, thick and luxuriant enough to hide a bird's nest. He had grown it when sailing the oceans as captain of a merchant ship transporting cargo to and from the Orient, and his experiences left him with a wealth of knowledge that Eric found useful in his chosen way of life. The tales he told, of strong nor-westerlies furrowing his eyebrows as he and his shipmates Rounded the Horn or braved the Good Hope, kept them warm on many a long winter evening. Old Yar had introduced him to his small band of friends, or landlubbers as he called them, all of whom could be trusted to help each other when they could and each with their own harrowing tales to tell.

Eric grew to respect each of them, especially a recent arrival in the group, Winnie, who was a tiny, motherly lady who carried her all her worldly goods in two carrier bags, one with 'Harvey Nichols' written on it and one advertising a shop called 'Argos'. She had wandered up from the city centre streets for a quieter life earlier in the year, away from the yobs that always chased her and threw rubbish at her as they shouted their taunts.

Winnie tutted quietly, but said nothing. Her unkempt grey hair was pulled back into a tatty knot, and a smudge of dirt was clearly visible on her cheek. Winnie was the nearest Eric had ever come to knowing a true bag lady, with no havens but a collection of carrier bags in which she took all her belongings with her everywhere. To cut down on the amount of baggage, she wore umpteen layers of vests, jumpers, scarves and coats, so that her appearance took on the proportions of a well-padded astronaut.

The younger man coughed slightly. Eric did not know him as well as he did the other two in the room, and he stiffened slightly in front of a relative stranger.

"Have you met Belt?" Winnie looked across at her companion, smiling.

The stranger smiled in return, showing a fine set of teeth with the two front ones missing, watching Eric on his rug. It was a strained smile, with dark, sad eyes, as if he were not used to stretching his face into that position, but I felt enough warmth behind his stiffness to think he was probably okay. His clothes were quite clean but scruffy, and the left shoe had a large hole in the toe. He wrapped his long legs into a knot as he curled up in the chair, clasping his knees with his arm. Winnie placed a hand on his lap and patted him gently.

"Belt's just come into town, from up country, like" she explained. She leaned forward and lowered her voice to a whisper. "He doesn't talk much, you'll find. In fact, he doesn't say anything. A bit shy, perhaps, or just checking us out first, I expect. But he's so true, Eric, don't you worry."

This confirmation was what Eric needed. If Winnie approved of a newcomer, then he must be all right. He decided to proceed with the reason for his visit.

"Actually," Eric said, casting his eyes around to include all of those present, "I do have something I need help with. Would you—I mean, do you mind?"

Old Yar sat upright, leaning forward.

"Let go aft, lad, and we'll do what we can."

Winnie and Belt nodded vigorously, and became alert, moving forward to the edge of their floppy chairs and watching him intently. Eric took a deep breath, and began to tell his tale. As he began, Thickpea scurried to a dark corner behind the leg of a chair, and settled to listen too, closely followed by two of her ratty mates.

6

She Said You'd Come

Eric's account of Bonnet's disappearance caused considerable anger amongst his small but enthralled audience. Old Yar's face, what could be seen of it behind the forest of white hair, went beetroot, his breath short and heavy. He lurched to his feet and paced the room urgently.

"A bad omen, leaving her hats, you know," he growled. "The lass felt undressed without them. She'll be in deep water now, no doubt."

"Oh, for goodness sake, give up on the sea references, will you?" It was rare for Winnie to lose her cool, especially in front of a stranger. "It's obvious what needs to be done, like. Eric, you say you know where she is?"

"I never said that," countered Eric. "A van skidded round the corner as I arrived back at the house—maybe that took her. I saw the young man, Blondie, head into a house backing onto the alleyway. 27 Pickering Avenue was the address. It's the only lead I've got. Whether Bonnet's in there or not, I can't say. I should have sent Thickpea," he added under his breath, annoyed with himself for not thinking of it at the time. "But it's not hard to find. I'll go back, see what I can do."

Old Yar coughed, as if trying to pluck up courage to say something momentous.

"I'd love to join you, boy," he explained, walking towards him with a pronounced limp in his left leg, "but my leg, you know, gored by that shark off East Africa ..."

Winnie chuckled.

"You needn't worry, old man, what with your dodgy pins and my asteroids, you and I aren't built for that kind of caper any more. Leave it to the youngster, he can cope."

Belt made a move and waved his hand to attract attention.

"You'll come?" Eric asked nervously. Belt nodded.

"I'm not sure that's a good idea," Winnie said, resting her hand on the man's knee. Leaning towards Eric, she added in a whisper, "I think he's a bit, you know, simple, not all there, a few pins short of a pin cushion. You should have seen him on bonfire night. Poor lad, really suffers with his swerves."

Eric looked at Belt, hoping he couldn't hear what the old woman was saying.

"Do you mean nerves?" he asked in a whisper.

A big frown swept across Winnie's wrinkled face.

"That's what I said, boy! You so need to clean your ears out. You know, a bit of a lipstick."

Eric hid a smile, then looked into Belt's eyes. His gaze was clear, with not a hint of dullness, confusion or fear. There was no problem there.

Belt returned the stare through the brownest eyes he had ever seen. They seemed to be liquid, were hard to focus on, but his brow was furrowed as he concentrated. He nodded reassuringly. Eric could see nothing to suggest that he was any pins short of anything.

"You said he's true, right?" He turned to Winnie.

She pulled herself up to her full but not great height.

"That's as may be, but—"

"Well, then he can come. But I want to go now, if that's okay."

Belt stood up immediately, picking up a tiny pile of rags and straightening his long, dark jacket to make himself more presentable to the outside world. Eric walked to the door, and he knew Thickpea wouldn't be far away. She scampered up as he made his way into the huge school hall on his way out of Hackney Mansions, Belt at his heels.

The walk to 27 Pickering Avenue was strangely silent. The only sounds were the two sets of footsteps as Eric and Belt walked quickly across the Downs, along the roads leading back towards Farthing Road. They kept up a good pace. Belt never spoke, walking a little behind Eric, who got the feeling he was keeping out of his line of sight. He gave the impression of not wanting to be looked at, a sensation Eric completely understood and sympathized with. Here was somebody he could make friends with, he began to hope; but knowing in his heart that homeless friends had a habit of disappearing. He thought of Doldrum, his first true friend after he found himself on the streets, and how she had left without warning, even though they had arranged to meet later that same day. He often wondered what had happened to her.

Eric and Belt kept away from busy streets, diving into alleyways whenever they could, even backtracking at one point when they realised they were reaching the shops near Stoke Newington. The people that dwelt around there disapproved of vagrants more than anywhere else on Eric's patch, so he kept out of direct contact with them as much as possible. The two of them ended up following the railway again, and Thickpea felt the boy relax physically as they left the road and went onto the embankment. It was harder going now, but the peace of mind made it worth it.

By the time Eric and Belt reached the alleyway that ran parallel to Pickering Avenue, it was getting dark. With so little time before Christmas, the nights were drawing in earlier every day, which helped their cause as they felt able to move more quickly in the gloom. Eric held out his arm, slowing Belt, and they crept up to a corner and peered into the alleyway. It was pitch black down there. No light reached them from the streetlights beyond the high fences. They made their way to the back gate of number 27, and stopped.

"Right," whispered Eric. "What now?"

Belt gestured to the gate.

"Go in?" Eric asked.

Belt nodded, then made a snake-like wriggle with his hand.
"Break in?"

Another nod. He separated his hands.

"We go in separately?"

Nod. Then pulled his hands together in a wide arc.

"And meet—where?"

Belt shrugged.

"No, silly me, we don't know what's in there yet. Look, you
stay downstairs, I'll do upstairs, and I'll meet you in the hall by
the front door. Okay?"

A final nod, then the young man gave a deep breath, reached
out and pushed open the gate. They went in, as quietly as they
could, picking their way through a mess of plant pots, piles of
empty cans and a fork that had been abandoned just where Eric
was about to put his foot. Belt grabbed him just in time.

"Thanks," breathed Eric, and Belt touched his arm reassuringly.

The back door was not locked, but opened with an ear-splitting creak that must have woken every neighbour within a mile
of the house. They paused, paralysed with fear, but nothing
happened. It seemed as though there was nobody at home.
Maybe this wasn't the house after all …

As they reached the long hallway, Eric and Thickpea headed
for the stairs and Belt made his way through a door on the right.
As he creaked his way up the staircase, Eric whispered to her.

"You do realise, my small hairy friend, that if there were
somebody in the house we would have been confronted by
now?"

So by the time they reached the top, Eric was no longer trying to be quiet.

There were three doors on the first floor landing. One stood wide open, revealing a bedroom with all the usual clutter. A scattering of dirty clothes was strewn on the floor, and there was the kind of smell you get when a window hasn't been opened for months. This was totally unlike number 7 Farthing Road, which was squeaky clean and untouched by human grime.

Nothing of interest here. Eric headed for the next door, which led to the bathroom—again a bit musty, and the tap dripped steadily into the grubby sink. Turning away, Eric froze. Standing in the final doorway was the shadow of a person, watching him.

"She was right then," said the figure. It was a young man's voice, not deep but still quite rich in tone, with a strong London accent. "She said it would be you who'd come."

Eric was stunned into silence. What was this person talking about? He tried to pick out any details he could see on the man's face. He was thin, with bandy legs and very short hair—he couldn't tell if it was blond, but he knew it would be. This was Blondie, Eric was certain.

"Well, let's get it sorted quickly, then. Come on, lad. No messing about. We got you. Give it up, kid."

The shadow moved forward, and Eric started out of his dreamy state. He dodged sideways with a loud yell, and headed for the stairs. He pelted down, closely followed by the man, who moved easily in the dark. This was a house he knew well.

"Don't be stupid, boy. Give it up, or I'll have to tie you."

He lunged at Eric, but missed and lost his balance, causing him to miss his footing. As Eric reached the bottom and skidded out of the way, the man fell to the floor, just as Belt came haring out of a doorway and landed on top of him. It was the man's turn to yell, but Belt sat tight. Thickpea leapt out of her pocket hideaway and ran straight to the man on the ground. Belt gasped.

"It's okay," Eric's voice was breathless as he turned and made to go back upstairs, "Thickpea's with me. I'll not be long," he panted in explanation for his dash back to the bedrooms. "Bonnet's in the last room, I'm sure of it."

With that he bounded upstairs two at a time and pulled open the third door. Again there was a musty, abandoned smell to the room, but a massive bed against the far wall showed Eric all he needed to know. More than enough, in fact. Bonnet was sitting hunched on the bedspread, her face streaked with tears and her hands firmly clasped on her bare head. She was terrified. Beside her, curled in a ball and vibrating like a car engine on tickover, was another child. Younger than Bonnet, and smaller in build, the girl slowly sat up and looked at Eric.

Eric gathered his thoughts—he had not expected to be rescuing two people—and took a deep breath.

"You okay?"

Both girls nodded, looking at each other for comfort.

"It's all right, I've come to get you out of here," the boy spoke softly, trying to keep the fear out of his voice. He did not know who else may be around, and wanted to get out of that house before they were discovered, otherwise they could all end up locked in there.

Bonnet gasped.

"Eric! Is that really you?"

She made to move closer to him, then suddenly jumped backwards and shrieked.

"Don't look at me! I'm naked!" She covered her head with her hands, and silent tears fell down her cheeks.

Eric took her gently by the arm and led her, not without some difficulty, downstairs. He would be back to fetch the other girl as soon as he could.

Belt was still using the man as a sofa, sprawled along his body as he tried to wriggle out of his grasp but his gaze was on Thickpea. The rat was staring at the man from just inches from his long face with pale, hollow cheeks. She had seen that face before; it was definitely Blondie, the man Eric and she had followed to the alleyway. Just as Bonnet had said, his features were pointed, the long nose separating a pair of piercing, hard, grey-blue eyes. The rat stood quite still, keeping her eyes firmly on her prey as if hypnotizing him. Eric took Bonnet past her captor and out of the house, then moments later reappeared and dashed up to get her other charge. When he had taken her outside too, ignoring Belt's amazed expression at finding an extra person, and the rat knew that Eric was safe, Thickpea moved suddenly. She bounded onto Blondie's head and scrabbled his scalp with her claws. Not something she enjoyed, playing in dandruff, but she would give herself a thorough clean later. Belt was shaking with silent laughter; then, as if it were planned, he grabbed the man's arms and pinned him to the ground.

Eric appeared in the doorway. Belt looked up enquiringly. Thickpea started a bit of minor scrabbling to keep the man occupied.

"She's fine," he said in reply to Belt's unspoken question. "What about him?"

Belt nodded to a table on which stood the telephone and a decorative lamp.

"Ring the police?"

He shook his head vigorously. Underworlders don't care to get involved with the police if they can help it. They tend to ask too many awkward questions. Thickpea was still doing her bit to help out, moving along his back this time, and heading for the line where his trousers were belted. A vigorous dig, to give the impression she wanted to bury herself down his trouser leg, certainly took his mind off the one-sided conversation behind him.

"Oh! The lamp. What, tie him up?"

Without waiting for Belt's confirmation, Eric reached for the lamp, unplugged it and took it to Belt. He clearly couldn't move, as the rat's attentions were causing their captive to wriggle more and more, and his hands were not the only part of him to be fully occupied. Eric reached over, wrapping the flex around Blondie's wrists, then pulled them tight to reach his ankles. It was a struggle, but eventually he was trussed like a turkey. Thickpea was proud of her helping tactics, but Belt was rubbing himself hard where he had been kicked and bruised by the wriggling man. A quick glance round and he found a filthy tea towel that he thrust into the blond man's mouth; then they all left the way they had come. The two girls were sitting by the front gate, shivering in the sharp winter chill, and Eric returned to the house to fetch a couple of blankets to warm them. He also found a yellow duster that Bonnet was able to fashion into a headscarf so that she no longer felt naked.

The young girl looked terrified as Eric and Belt came out to join her. Her eyes were wide and round, her body tense, and her movements stiff, even though she had not been tied up or imprisoned for long. She backed away as Belt reached her.

"I'm Eric," said the boy, careful not to get too close to her and frighten her even more, "and this is Belt. You've met Bonnet, I see."

Belt grinned, and the lass seemed to soften, her fear turning to exhaustion as she crumpled on the ground, too tired to run or hide. Belt knelt beside her, and gently touched her hand. Then, to Eric's great surprise, he spoke.

"I never believed I would see you again," he whispered, and Eric noticed for the first time a tear trickling down his cheek. "You need have no fear of the boy, my darling. He helped me find you. He's daddy's friend."

The girl looked into his chocolate brown eyes, and it was as though a veil was lifted from her sight. She recognized him, and a huge smile transformed the frightened little waif into a lovely, brown-eyed daughter in the arms of a father she feared she would never see again. They hugged so tightly that Thickpea was afraid they would crush each other, but all she felt was a warm glow from the love they were giving each other in their embrace. Eric turned to Bonnet, who was still sitting on the floor, her mouth open, her gaze fixed on the two reunited people in front on her.

"He's okay, Bonnet, Winnie said he was true—and he came with me to get you," Eric reassured her, "and now I know why." Eric felt Thickpea fidgetting.

"Let's get out of here," he urged, standing up quite suddenly. "I can hear—"

The sound of a vehicle approaching grew louder. They tensed, and threw themselves in an untidy heap into the shadow of a neighbouring gateway as a dirty white van pulled up outside the house they had just left, and a man dashed up the drive and into the front door. They had left it wide open. They needed no persuading to move on swiftly now, listening out constantly for the sound of a van following them.

Belt and his daughter accompanied Eric, Thickpea and Bonnet as far as the railway station. There he turned to them and shook them warmly by the hand.

"I will return to see you again, Eric," he said, the dark eyes brimming with tears, "and I will explain everything. In the meantime, if there is ever anything you need—"

He reached inside his jacket and pulled out a small piece of card, handing it to Eric.

"This is my number, and you can get in touch any time. You helped me get my daughter back. I owe you more than I can ever repay, Eric. Anything, any time. Remember."

Eric was touched by his affection and concern for his safety.

"Tell me one thing before you go," he said, pocketing the card in Thickpea's pocket nest, "What is you daughter's name?"

Belt smiled and looked lovingly down at the young girl held firmly in his arms.

"Yes, of course, where are my manners? Eric, may I introduce Ellie. Ellie, this is Eric. Who knows, one day maybe you'll become good friends."

With that, Belt and Ellie walked onto the station platform just as a train for Liverpool Street Station pulled in, and they made their way onto the carriage and out of sight.

7

Paprika Stew

The rescue party's welcome at the Mansions was rapturous.
Winnie was the first to greet them, with a cry of relief and the

closest thing Eric had ever seen to a human tsunami—floods of tears, quite wasted, he thought, as they were all perfectly safe; then Old Yar strode forward, arms outstretched, his bearlike embrace almost squashing Thickpea as she snuggled in Eric's pocket.

"Oh, my girl, we've been so worried," Winnie fussed about, brushing the hair from Bonnet's face, and smoothing her cheeks as if finishing a fine sculpture. "All sorts of awful pictures were forming in my head. You could have been assorted, or beaten with a cod."

The others turned and stared at the old woman at this amazing pronouncement, and Thickpea was sure she could hear their brains whirring as they tried to work out what she meant by it.

"Er, do you mean a cosh, old lass?" ventured Old Yar rather nervously. He knew that Winnie had a firm belief in her verbal accuracy and was not keen on being corrected.

Her expression as black as thunder, Winnie whisked Bonnet away to get her cleaned up and calmed down, while Eric was swept by the old seaman into a comfortable armchair in the old staff room and made to recount the adventure.

Eric told his tale well, and managed to miss out any bits about Thickpea.

"Well done, my boy," Old Yar beamed at him. "I'm proud of you. And that lubber, what's his name, he did well too. Where has he gone?"

"I couldn't have done it without Belt," admitted Eric, his hands clasping an old tin can that contained a dribble of rum out of Old Yar's precious flask. "If Belt hadn't come in with me, to grab Blondie, I'd have been caught and the girls still imprisoned. I hope he doesn't vanish for good," he added ruefully, thinking again of his dear Doldrum and her sudden departure.

Belt had left too many unanswered questions to vanish for good. Eric was certain he would see his new friend again.

Winnie came back into the staff room with Bonnet, now clean and smart but still snivelling. Winnie was rubbing her hands on her rag dangling from her waist. Bonnet walked behind her, her face lowered, eyes scanning the floor.

"Are you alright?" Eric asked her.

Bonnet glanced up at him, and nodded. Winnie sniffed.

"I'm not sure she is. I think she's going down with rhine-stone-itis."

Everybody froze, but only for a moment. Winnie always found medical terms a bit tricky; but this was a new one.

"Rhinitis," murmured Eric quietly, realizing what she had meant. They all relaxed.

"Good Lord, it's well past eight bells," declared Old Yar with a forced cheerfulness. "It's time to sling out the hammocks before we drop to the deck. Then tomorrow, I think we deserve a bit of seasonal merriment, don't you? How about a voyage into town to see the lights?"

"I think that maybe Bonnet could do with a rest rather than an excursion," said Winnie after a moment's thought. "I'll stay and look after her. You two boys go and enjoy yourselves."

Cheered and quite exhausted, they all made for different rooms, piled up a collection of blankets and cushions into beds, and snuggled down, Eric and Thickpea looking forward to the promise of a diversion in the morning.

Six Days To Christmas

As Christmas approached, the streets around the Stoke Newington shops were bedecked with decorations, their front windows colourfully stocked with ideas for presents and festive treats. A string of fairy lights hung from every lamppost, and above the street swung sleighs, reindeer and snowmen shaped out of bulbs. Old Yar and Eric joined the crowds of Saturday shoppers with their hum of expectancy, all hopeful of finding a perfect present for somebody, and having a bit of fun in the process. They were not used to the pavements being that busy, preferring to keep out of the way during normal shopping hours for fear of attracting the attention of the yobs and louts that took delight in taunting and harassing them. Today, they did not care. This was a treat. This was not a time for hiding in the shrubbery. Eric strode out purposefully, his head held high, as Old Yar rolled along with his sailor's rolling swagger of a walk.

Some of the trees in the front gardens they passed were swathed in light strings, with a succession of colours running along like shooting stars chasing each other, switched on even in broad daylight. Every window had been decorated with great care, the reds, greens and golds of the season echoed in the baubles and tinsel, even in the display of Advent Buns in the local bakery, topped with glittery messages of Yuletide joy. The pavements were full of shoppers, staring at the goods on offer and choosing their own Christmas delights. Old Yar and Eric wore their best clothes, including a red Father Christmas hat that kept Old Yar's ears warm. They wandered along, eyes wide, mouths open, soaking up the Christmas atmosphere. The shoppers were so busy, they didn't even have time to stare rudely at them, or to move away deliberately as if they were infectious. It made the two men almost feel as if they belonged.

Eric was quite fascinated by the way people shopped. Some seemed to stand and stare, taking an age to decide what they really wanted to spend their money on; while others stopped suddenly as they saw something in a window, dashing in to buy it before somebody else did. Older people with a single shopping bag might buy no more than it took to fill it, whereas the younger ones ended up laden with armfuls of carrier bags as they made their weary way home.

Old Yar strode out as if the town were his demesne, like an overlord striding through his estate. His back straight, his magnificently white head of hair held high, his arms swinging rhythmically as he moved, he scanned the road ahead as if searching for a potential pirate attack. He was an impressive figure and only his clothing gave away his lifestyle, with his best, or rather, least ragged, overcoat tied at the waist with a length of bright orange plastic string and a pair of filthy Wellington boots striding out. Eric knew he had a rather changeable attitude to rats, as he hated the idea of them running loose around Hackney Mansions, but he seemed to tolerate Thickpea's presence, as long as she was sensible enough to stay out of his reach. She remained in her pocket, sneaking an occasional glance out of the hole she had picked in the seam as they walked along.

Thickpea's first encounter with Eric had been the previous spring, as a young animal on one of her first forays into the big wide world. Her many companions and she were leaving the shelter of the Stoke Newington tunnel after their first few weeks of life, used to the dark, grimy world under ground, now smelling the fresh air for the first time. As they sneaked round the edge of the pillar that held the end arch of the tunnel, they were startled to a full stop by the bright light. Blinking rapidly; they had no idea where it came from, but it made sense. Why else had they been given eyes? As each creature became accustomed to the daylight, they began to notice the other more subtle characteristics of life above ground. There was no roof, for a start. Far above them was an empty blue space, frightening in its vastness, but clearly not dangerous, as every now and then they saw creatures—they learned later that they were pigeons—swooping and flapping noisily overhead. In front, beside the tracks of the railway, were steep banks of long, tatty grasses dotted with other leafy growths, and at the top of the green slopes were the damp, shiny brown roofs of buildings on the roads running parallel to the line, their long straight lines broken up by the chimneys on which the pigeons landed and cooed at each other. There was so much to see, so many new sensations to take in, that Thickpea and her friends were momentarily off their guard, and that was the first rule they had to learn the hard way. Suddenly, without warning, a loud screech issued from a flying ball of fur that launched itself from the long grass, landing in the midst of them and right on top of one unfortunate young rat. The cat pounced with vicious suddenness, biting it through the neck so quickly that he was killed instantly; then it sat, a smug look on its face, watching as young rats scattered in terror, its prey lying dead under its front paws.

Most of the ratlings scrambled back into the dark mouth of the tunnel, to the safety they were familiar with, but in her panic Thickpea bolted in the opposite direction. She could hear the wild screams from the rest of them, but the sounds were getting fainter as she headed for the grass in the hope of finding refuge. Her breath was coming in loud gasps by the time she burrowed into the roots of the soft, green foliage, and she lay still, waiting for panic to leave her alone and calm to return, and slowly she felt her pounding heart quieten

After a while, the young rat became aware of a strangely familiar sensation seeping through her. She was hungry. Her nose, overwhelmed by the new scents that surrounded her, had picked up an inkling of a trail, something pleasant, that made her mouth water, and she lifted her head to assess the direction she had to follow. Then, gingerly at first, she made her way, clump by clump, towards a small, square, brown box, and carefully sniffed. Yes, that was definitely the source of the scent. A quick look round, then Thickpea pushed under a flap of card and was inside, with no further dallying, the instinct to eat stronger than any fear of the unknown—one of the pointers that showed her to be a young rat, without the experience to tell her to be more wary.

In a dim corner of the box was a lump of something hard and yellow, which had a very strong smell, and an investigative nibble told her it tasted wonderful. It was cheese. Then, the box started to move. It seemed to float, wobbling so much that Thickpea could not stand still, but slid from side to side as she was carried away. The trap had worked; she had already lost her freedom.

She had no idea how long the box was moving. By the time the lurching ended, she was quite disorientated, not knowing which way up she was, let alone where she was. The movement stopped, and everything went quiet. Then a fresh lump of something edible was pushed carefully through the flap, so as not to allow enough space for the rat to make a run for it, and all went peaceful for a long time. She did not approach the new food at first—it took some time before her stomach felt steady enough to take food—but again instinct took over, and it did smell delicious. It was soft, brown, and had holes in it—Thickpea came to know it as bread—and although it was a bit dry, it helped her settle after her ordeal.

Her brain clicked into gear as she realized that although she was a prisoner, she had a benefactor, somebody who was looking after her, maybe somebody who had saved her life by taking her away from that flying cat at the tunnel mouth. It was strange; Thickpea did not feel scared, more excited, to meet a new friend, to see who it was that wanted her as a—well, she didn't know what for. That was the worrying bit, to be honest.

It was some time before Thickpea saw Eric. He kept her in the box for some days, supplying food and a little water on a leaf from time to time, and she got used to her surroundings. She heard sounds from outside, often a quiet muttering, as she got her used to his voice. Then, one day, the flap opened, and stayed open. The young rat sat quite still. Was it a trap? How safe was it out there? But nothing happened for a while, until the muttering started again.

"You're alright, you know," he murmured gently, "I'm Eric, I'll look after you, and in a while I'll let you go back. You'll be fed, we'll have adventures, I'll show you new places and teach you all I can. Come on, let's have a look at you."

Thickpea's curiosity got the better of her. She stuck her nose out, half expecting that cat to pounce; but no, there was no cat in sight. Instead she saw a boy, squatting on the ground in front of her, his arms hugging his knees, his eyes watching her intently. He spoke again.

"Well, hello there," he said, a little grin on his face.

She snuffled towards him, hesitantly, watching for any sudden motion that meant danger, yet there was a calm stillness about the boy that soothed her nerves and within a short time any trace of fear had evaporated. From then on their friendship developed at a momentum that took them both by surprise. Within days the rat would sit on his knee, eat out of his fingers, even snuffle her nose through his hair as a sign of affection. This was an emotion she had not experienced before, and she liked it. This boy became her reason and her purpose, as well as her best mate.

It was this part of their history that filled Thickpea's mind as they wandered through a Christmassy Stoke Newington. She felt privileged to be with everyone there, and without thinking, stuck her head out with pride, breathing in the rich scents of coffee, the fresh bread, and the perfumed odours given off by most of the women and quite a few of the men—until the peace was shattered by a shrill cry close by.

"Aaaaaaah!"

Everybody looked round. An elderly lady, with a flat, round hat perched on her head and an umbrella held upright as a weapon, was staring at Eric's chest.

"A rat! It's a RAT!!!"

The crowds stopped, stared, then parted to let the two men through as quickly as possible, and rather sheepishly they left the main street. Old Yar's haughty manner was crushed, as he held his head low, trying but failing to be invisible. Eric pushed Thickpea's head down and wrapped his jacket a little closer as he walked swiftly away.

"Good move, Thickpea," he whispered sharply, "How to win friends and influence people. You'll never be a hit among those among us who wash every day, you know that, don't you?"

Thickpea felt ashamed. She burrowed deeper, and stayed out of sight; at least she could peek out through the seam of the pocket without being seen.

A rumble of wheels betrayed the arrival of Kal and the Fractured Jawbone gang. The crowds on the pavement parted with people grumbling under their breath at the unthinking youth of today, and five boys on skateboards clattered by. They were plugged in to earphones, and seemed totally oblivious to everybody else on the street. Eric had felt an urge to hide, but the crush of shoppers kept him where he stood. He instinctively put his hand up to Thickpea's pocket, hiding her from view. He need not have worried. The gang paid no heed to him, or his pocket, or to anybody else.

A short distance from the High Street stood Mr Burgonya's greengrocery, a tiny building amongst taller houses, more like a garden shed than a place of enterprise. It was fronted with a green awning under which Mr Burgonya laid out all his goods, a colourful array of fruit and vegetables that were one of the most inviting and mouth-watering sights Eric had seen for many long, cold days. There, standing just inside the doorway, waiting to greet each customer personally, was Mr Burgonya.

He was one of the most remarkable men Eric had met in the four years he had spent in the vagrant life. His immense height meant he had to duck beneath the lintel to get through the door, and when he did his thin, lanky body seemed to slither rather than walk. As he ducked, his head came into full view. His hair was a shocking red, and had never been tamed by comb or brush. Winnie had told Eric that whenever she saw him, her hands always reached for the comb she carried in a pocket, in the hope that Mr Burgonya would allow her to attack the fiery mop that topped the ruddy complexion which encompassed his snub nose and soft, dark eyes. Apparently, in her own words, she was afraid he suffered from headlines.

A wide beam lit the greengrocer's face as he saw them approaching.

"Why, my dear friends!" he gushed, arms outstretched, reaching them in a couple of huge strides. "Welcome, in you come, my house is your house, always welcome!"

Old Yar smiled back, nodding sagely, and ushered Eric before him into the shop. It was warm compared to the seasonal cool outside, and there was a comforting scent of vegetables, earth and spices. Mr Burgonya followed, arms still wide, guiding the two of them deep into the shadowy interior like a couple of sheep being coaxed back to the rest of the flock. When they were all safely under cover, he shouted upstairs.

"Magdalena! Come, out front, take care of the shop!"

The sound of footsteps heralded the arrival of a young girl with the same shock of red hair as her father and a long, flowing skirt. She made her way outside, her father pushing the shop door closed behind her.

"So long, my friends, since you came here. You must eat. Come!"

Judging by the food Mr Burgonya pressed on Eric, he must have thought they had not fed at all since their last visit. Before he even sat down around the large, round table, the greengrocer had clapped his hands and commanded a massive range of dishes to be laid out before them both. A woman scurried out from the kitchen at the back, smiling and rubbing her hands together, and bowed her head at every request. Mrs Burgonya was the opposite of her husband—short and round, with her hair in a tight bun and huge spectacles that made her eyes as large as chocolate chip cookies. Her husband spoke to her in her own language, but it was not hard to guess the meaning of his instructions. Out of the kitchen as if by magic came a succession of dishes, full to the brim with rich, spicy stew, potatoes cooked with hot, filling-melting paprika, and bowls overflowing with several mixed crunchy salads, along with piles of freshly baked bread and a bowl full of butter, a luxury Thickpea had never seen before.

"Eat! Eat! Then you tell me your news."

Well, with such insistence, how could they refuse? Old Yar piled mountains of hot, spicy stew, potatoes with paprika, green leafy salad and malty brown bread onto his plate, but Eric took small amounts onto his own, knowing that his stomach was not used to the rich flavours. Thickpea sneaked out of Eric's pocket and onto his lap, where the boy managed to pass her tiny morsels of food, which she tried to eat as quietly as she could. Rats are not known to be particularly quiet, or polite, eaters, so it was not easy, but nobody screamed, so she reckoned she must have managed it.

There followed a long period of knives and forks clattering, contented munching noises from the diners, and occasional snippets of "Mmmm!" and "This is lovely, Mrs Burgonya," whenever a mouth was empty enough to speak. It was after all the plates had been wiped clean and all traces of juice mopped up by lumps of bread, that Mr Burgonya seemed satisfied, and let his wife remove the plates from the table. She vanished into the kitchen and was soon rattling the dishes as she washed up, and her husband brought out a tall, thin bottle containing a clear, syrupy liquid, along with three glasses, and for the first time joined us at the table. It was time to talk.

8

Flying Carrots

Before Old Yar could begin to tell Mr Burgonya our news, they all had to sit through the usual routine; the old Hungarian would relive his life story as if he were telling it for the first time. Thickpea snuggled down on Eric's lap and dozed. She had heard it all before, several times.

Mr Burgonya had been born on a farm close to the Hungar-ian city of Budapest, in a place he described as the most beauti-ful spot in the world. Its history is reflected in its buildings, dating from before the time when the two halves of the city were separate, only becoming a mighty centre of life and com-merce after they were joined together. Since then its chequered saga of war and upheaval had strengthened it, while retaining a beauty and stature that bound it to its inhabitants.

Mr Burgonya's parents and six elder brothers lived in the farmhouse until one by one the boys grew up, married, and built a new house of their own on the farm land. The river Danube flowed close by, flooding the land in winter, making it fertile and productive, so the family could make a good living growing potatoes, a staple food among the local people. But the land was changing. Their closeness to Budapest meant that the air and river were becoming polluted by waste from the chemi-cal factories that lined its banks upstream and the growing number of people living at the fringes of the city, and over the years their crops had become weaker and thinner as the land was slowly poisoned. Mr Burgonya's had been a happy childhood blighted by one fact; his health was poor, and he spent a great deal of time lying on his bed wheezing and weak, watching the others tending the crops, looking after the livestock and doing the chores. His mother blamed the foul air that resulted from factories belching out smoke and filth on the outskirts of the city; so when he reached the age where he could make his own decisions, he left his beloved home and headed for England, hoping he would find cleaner air and a better chance of a healthy lifestyle that would enable him to make his own living. If he made a good living, he would send money back to his fam-ily to help them out.

It took time to get established in London, and for a while Mr Burgonya found himself living on the streets, scavenging for scraps and sleeping under the arches close to Liverpool Street Station. Whilst there he met Old Yar, who helped him learn how to survive, and who encouraged him to continue with his quest to use his experience and run a little greengrocer's shop. Old Yar helped him find work at the vegetable market on Portabello Road, coaching him for the brief interview and teaching him basic English. As his earnings increased with his experience, he was able to achieve his ambition, and after years of toil and difficulty, he ended up in Stoke Newington, providing fruit and vegetables for the well-to-do who lived there. His experiences explained his attitude to vagrants; he was exceedingly grateful to the old sailor who had helped him during a time of need, and was always willing to repay in any way he felt able.

Then he met Mrs Burgonya, or, as she was then known, Miss Krumpli. Eric loved the names. Mr Burgonya told him that both his name, and his wife's maiden name, meant potato in Hungarian. She had been working for some years in a large household in London as a cook, and their paths crossed when Mr Burgonya supplied the fresh produce for the large dinner parties cooked by his future wife. Without a second thought, they married, she left her employment and the two of them moved into the flat above the shop. His knowledge of quality and buying, matched with hers of managing food and money, led their business to flourish.

By the time he had finished his reminiscences the Hungarian greengrocer was shedding tears, and Old Yar leaned over to comfort him with an arm around his shoulders,

"A fine yarn, my old landlubber," he said soothingly, "that gets better every time you tell it. And look at you now! A successful businessman, with strong ballast to keep you safe, a lovely wench to look after you and good food in your belly. What more can a man want?"

It was his usual answer at this point, and provoked the expected response. Mr Burgonya sniffed hard, blew his long, thin nose with a pure white handkerchief, and rose to his feet.

"You are right, as always, my seafaring friend," he leaned over, pouring the last of the bottle into the sailor's glass. "And here am I taking up your time with my woes, when you must have so much to tell me. Now, it is your turn!"

This was the signal for Old Yar to begin to relate the latest news and adventures, filling in his host with all the wrinkles of vagrant life. My Burgonya loved to hear every detail, maybe because he was relieved to have moved back into a house, but Eric thought it was also with due respect to Old Yar.

Thickpea gave a shake, and took the opportunity to sneak away and explore the shop. A good rummage led to some tasty discoveries—a few overripe grapes in need of clearing up, a banana skin which had not been scraped clean, even a few pomegranate seeds with their thick layer of sweet, pink flesh on them, just waiting to be eaten. It was her duty to help out, cleaning up after being given such a tasty meal—so she did. While she munched, she leapt onto the counter, and watched the shoppers passing by on the pavement.

The sky was darkening at the end of another Christmas shopping day. At the front of the shop, where the boxes of fruit and vegetables were being tended by Magdalena, a flurry of people were buying odd pieces of fruit and veg. An old gentleman with a pink shopping bag was waving an umbrella at what he wanted, while Magdalena carefully put his chosen items into a bag. He was followed by a couple of ladies wearing headscarves, who purchased two grapefruit and a pound of dates. The rat watched through the glass, licking her paws and rubbing her whiskers to keep them in top condition. Then she felt a cold shiver run down her spine, and she saw something that made her freeze.

A young man was approaching the shop. His face was lowered, but a long, pointed nose protruded from the shadows and his head was crowned in cropped blond hair. It was Blondie, Bonnet's abductor, no doubt about it. Thickpea's anger bubbled up, and she squealed at the top of her voice; and that was quite loud enough to wake a sleeping rat two houses away. The door flew open, and Eric flew out, followed by the others. They saw the rat staring out of the window at the young man, now intent on buying a bag of apples.

"Nice one, Thickpea," said Eric, thinking fast. It was not a good idea for Thickpea to be seen there. He scooped her up in his hand, stuffing her rather unceremoniously into her pocket, leaving her to untangle her legs and tail herself. Then, beckoning urgently to Old Yar, he headed for the front door. It opened with the customary jingle and before Blondie could react, Eric had grabbed him by the arm and pulled him into the shop. He had no time to respond, shocked by the suddenness of Eric's actions, but as his eyes grew accustomed to the dim interior of the shop, his wits clicked into focus.

"Here, what's all this?" he said angrily, looking round at each face in turn. Mr Burgonya was standing back, keeping out of the way, unsure what was going on but reluctant to intervene. Old Yar was staring at the young man with a look of distinct loathing on his face, though without a clue what the man was supposed to have done wrong—stolen a cabbage, perhaps, or pilfered another man's rum ration. Mrs Burgonya came bustling in from the kitchen to see what all the fuss was about, and when she saw the young man in front of them, she hid behind her husband, clearly terrified by what she saw. But when Blondie's glance reached Eric, he stopped and met the boy's angry stare. The cold eyes began to register a shimmer of fear in Thickpea's thick fur.

"You!" he breathed heavily, then turned on the spot and tried to make a bolt for the door. Thickpea decided her rough handling had given her a right to react. She leapt from her pocket with a loud squeal, landing on the arm of Blondie's coat. The man looked down and yelled, remembering their previous meeting when Thickpea had pinned him to the ground in the hall of 27 Pickering Avenue. He shook his arm violently to try and remove her. He nearly managed it, too—but not quite. It was enough to stop his flight, and Eric and Old Yar rushed forward to restrain him by the shoulders. They pushed him to a chair and made him sit, and crowded closer to prevent him getting away.

"Well?" Old Yar found his voice, despite puffing a bit with the exertion. "Who is this then, boy?"

Eric snarled.

"He was the one who took Bonnet."

The old sailor roared his rage and moved forward as if to strike the man. Eric stepped between them, and Old Yar's anger vanished as quickly as it came.

"No, we need answers," said Eric, arms held wide and trying to explain what he wanted now they had the man in their custody. "We need to know what's going on. "You!" His voice sounded much braver than he felt. "Why did you kidnap my friend?"

As he spoke he stared at Blondie, who was still agitated by Thickpea's presence on the arm of his coat, sweeping his hand up and down his sleeve to get rid of her. She simply moved out of the way each time, but refused to loosen her grip. Mr Burgonya was beginning to get agitated himself, at the thought of what the Health and Safety people would say if they knew he had a rat in his shop.

In his distressed state, Blondie looked ready to tell them whatever we wanted to know. He spoke quickly, as if he couldn't get the words out fast enough. His pale eyes looked ghostly with panic. Eric was a little surprised at his obvious fear—for a young man capable of such bravado and swagger when he was on the street, he seemed to have crumpled into a gibbering wreck with hardly any effort on their part.

"The guv'nor wanted you," he gabbled, nodding towards Eric, "she knew you would come—get this thing off my arm—I didn't want anything to do with it, for pity's sake—get it away!—just wanted you to get the blame, to be found with her, to be in trouble with the cops. Look, I hate rats, get it away from me, I can't tell you any more unless—"

While he spoke, his voice became more and more disjointed as his agitation grew. He was clearly in a great deal of distress. Eric almost took pity on him.

"Thickpea," he said reprovingly, and held out his hand. Reluctantly she left her post, climbing up his arm and into her pocket. But she kept a careful eye on Blondie through the ripped seam. As she vanished from view, Mr Burgonya let out a long, low breath of relief.

"Better?" said Eric harshly. He had little sympathy with anybody who did not like rats, so his goodwill towards this young man could not sink much lower. But as Blondie relaxed, their captive began to talk more easily.

"Ta, mate," he said, visibly sagging in the chair.

Old Yar was muttering under his breath.

"It wasn't like this in my day. A powder monkey knew his place on my ship, I can tell you."

Nobody was listening.

Blondie seemed to gather his thoughts, then began to tell his tale.

"You, boy, seem to be quite a catch, but I can't tell you why. It's more than my life's worth. You needed to be discredited, to show how you can't be trusted, up to no good, in with a bad lot—all that, see? My job was to get you in a compromising position, and then I would be out of it."

"But why?" Eric was bewildered, with no idea what the man was referring to. "Why me? What's so special about me? And who's she?"

"Look, I'm just a nobody, doing stuff for a living, that's all. If it's a bit dodgy, then it's not me, it's the people who give me the job, right? I don't know nothing you want, okay? It's the guvnor you need to speak to, not me. He'll tell you all you need to know."

"The guvnor? Who's the guvnor? Who else is involved in all this? What's going on?"

Blondie shuffled uncomfortably.

"I shouldn't have said anything. You don't have to know that. It's not important. I'm just helping out, okay? I get paid for this, that's all. Then we're out of it. Look, the girl's alright, ain't she? I never touched her, never had to. She just huddled up in a ball and yelped a lot about being naked. But she wasn't. I never touched her clothes, or anything else, honest."

Eric repeated his questions twice more, but Blondie was determined not to give anymore away. This seemed to be getting nowhere now, and Eric and the sailor moved back. Mr Burgonya was looking anxiously out of the window. It was nearly time to shut the shop—they had been there most of the afternoon.

The answer came from Blondie. Taking advantage of their slight relaxation, he made an unexpected lurch at the door, flung it open, bumped into Magdalena, knocking a handful of carrots she had in her hand flying into the air, and fled, haring towards High Street where the last minute shoppers still thronged the pavements. Eric and his friends stood in stunned silence. The door hung open, Magdalena stood open-mouthed staring at them, and the air hung with a dull, strange quiet as they all let the events of the afternoon sink in. Blondie had vanished into the gloomy street, any sound of his footsteps drowned by the distant rumble of rush-hour traffic making its way home.

Old Yar was the first to speak.

"My dear old turbot,"—his affectionate name for the greengrocer—"this has been most trying for you. Let us leave you to calmer waters while we tack for home."

Eric and Old Yar took their leave, with Thickpea safely tucked in his pocket. Mr Burgonya insisted on pressing a box of slightly overripe fruit as a seasonal gift into his old friend's hands, and begged them both to return whenever they were passing. Thickpea picked up vibrations of fear and a touch of annoyance in him as they left; she got the feeling the Hungarian greengrocer didn't actually mean that bit.

The return journey to Hackney Mansions was uneventful. Eric and Old Yar kept an eye out for Blondie but without success. The whole episode had been quite baffling. The journey was completed in total silence as the boy tried to come up with some answers.

9

Taking Stock

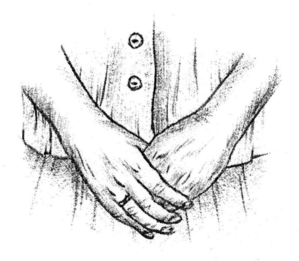

Hackney Mansions looked dour and sombre after dark. Its windows, long since empty of glass, were like eye sockets, allowing its black soul to stare out. Every doorway was littered with dead leaves, rubbish blown in over years of neglect, and a thick layer of earthy dust. Eric had to pick his way through it all carefully. Its dilapidated state had attracted a range of social outcasts from time to time, from gangs of young lads like Kal's who wrecked whatever they found, to true Romany's with their caravans, untrained dogs and what seem like dozens of children chasing, screaming and whooping along the corridors. It was not a secret place, set as it was on a large plot of land right next to the railway, and in clear view from all the commuters heading for and from the city twice a day; but the few rooms used by Old Yar and his friends were away out of direct sight in a far corner of the main building. Overlooking what used to be the main driveway and the playground, it afforded an excellent point to see who was approaching, and left the inhabitants ample time to make a getaway, or at least make for a better hiding place within the grounds, usually the huge basement, reached by a narrow staircase hidden behind a pile of old filing cabinets.

Old Yar made his way up a rickety staircase to a tiny cupboard he used as a bedroom, grumbling that he didn't have a hammock to sleep in. Nobody heard him. Eric entered the old school staff room as a scurry of movement from the next room, an old cloakroom, heralded the arrival of Bonnet. She wore a Wee Willie Winkie nightcap, and rhythmic snores were coming from a pile of blankets further into the shadows. Bonnet came closer, her finger to her lips.

"Hush, now, don't you wake her," she whispered, waving her hand towards the blankets that rose and fell with Winnie's breathing. "I sang her a lullaby, and she is sleeping at last. I told her that daddy's going to buy her a mocking bird, and if it doesn't sing, a diamond ring, and if it turns out to be brass, he'll get her a looking glass, and if—"

"Yes, right," interrupted Eric, getting the general idea. "What about you? How do you feel?"

"Shhh!" Bonnet ushered him back, trying to keep him quiet. "I'll tell you over there. Hang on, I need to change—"

She reached for her hat bag and pulled out the deerstalker, replacing the nightcap on her head. "Anyway, as I was saying, if the looking glass—what am I saying? Stick to facts, eliminate the impossible, and whatever is left, however improbable, will be the answer."

"Right," Eric turned to walk to a soft chair by a window. "Just what I was about to say. Now, are you ready? Tell me everything, from the beginning."

"Well," Bonnet settled herself in a heap on the floor by Eric's chair. "It was just after you left to follow that other young fellow-me-lad, as I was keeping an eye on the house. I had just decided to have a doze, when the front door opened and a woman came out. Grey hair, a really tight grip, wrinkly stockings. She grabbed me, and pulled me inside, leaving all my belongings all over the front garden. No respect for possession, I ask you."

"A woman? Thin? Fat? Bald?"

"Well, she was short and round—"

"You mean fat?"

"Well, no, more—cuddly, if you know what I mean."

"Okay," Eric smiled. "Go on."

Bonnet screwed up her face as she concentrated.

"With a neat bun of grey hair. Her face was made up with some care, and she carried herself like a lady. Her hands were not working hands, no callouses or rough skin, and she wore a gold ring on her right hand, with a rope effect twisted round it as decoration. I was blindfolded, then somebody else came and the two of them manhandled me into a vehicle, with big doors and a bench seat—probably a van. I passed the time trying to work out if the van had radial tyres or four-ply. Or is that wool? Anyway, the journey was short, plenty of corners, judging by the way we were bounced from side to side. Then I was bundled out, through a front door, up a flight of stairs, carpeted—I could tell by the sound we made—and dumped on a bed. My hood was pulled off, but it was dark, closed curtains, no light, and my captors left immediately. They never spoke at all. I didn't see the other person, could have been male or female. That's about it, I'm afraid."

"Well, it'll have to do," answered Eric, as usual quite stunned at the amount of detail Bonnet considered a poor description. "But we have more to add." He went on to tell her about following Blondie to the house in the alleyway, at which point she started nodding vigorously.

"Yes, that's it! A grim little place, no real class, a building of low quality and in a mediocre area of town."

Eric continued and Bonnet flinched when he reached the part where she had considered herself naked.

"But there's more," the boy continued urgently. "We saw him, Blondie, later on, at the shops." He continued his tale, and the girl's eyes grew wider as the story progressed.

"I see," she said thoughtfully, her lips pursed, her brow furrowed. "A Mystery. Good. I was only telling Doctor Watson the other day that I need a stimulating case to exercise my intellect. This other man who assisted you, Belt, was it? He gave no idea of his true identity before he spoke?"

Eric shook his head.

"I see. He must have had some inkling that his daughter was close by, and that acting the role of a vagrant would find her. I wonder why. I am sure we will see him again, old friend. But for now, I need rest. Come, boy, time for bed. You've had a trying day, and need to recharge your little grey cells. Hang on—"

She reached into her bag again and pulled out a mouldy bowler hat. She removed the deerstalker, replacing it with what Thickpea thought looked like an out-of-date plum pudding. The change in her demeanour was immediate. She sat up primly and gave a tight-lipped smile.

"Yes, Hastings, my faithful English bloodhound," she murmured, with a very good foreign accent, "my little grey cells are in need of recuperation, no?"

With that, she scooped up her bag and with a mincing walk, went back to her cloakroom.

10

Storm Brewing

Five Days to Christmas

The following morning dawned brighter. The damp weather had broken, leaving a clear blue sky hanging over a newly washed city. But the dry brought with it a cold that nibbled at toes, fingers and nose, letting everybody know winter was well on the way and this was only a taste of what was to come.

It had been a disturbed night for Eric. Bonnet twitched and yelped her way through a series of nightmares in which she must have relived her horrific experiences of the past days; and the only person woken by them was Eric. Winnie slept in her corner of the cloakroom, where she had laid herself down the evening before, reaching a depth of sleep that must have been close to a coma, and Old Yar's snores echoed down from his broom cupboard like distant thunder. Eric tossed and turned, his head full of the stories he had heard, wondering how much he could take in at any one time. Was he really the reason for Bonnet's abduction, and if so, why? Blondie had said Eric needed to be discredited; so he must have upset somebody, somehow, and he had not a clue how. And who was Blondie, anyway? He seemed very keen not to reveal his identity, that was sure. Thickpea watched the boy, lying wrapped in his blanket, body tense, eyes open, clearly wide awake, and crept out of her pocket and onto his chest. He reached up with his hand and stroked her back.

"I think I need some time out, my friend," he whispered.

The rat knew what that meant. Whenever he needed to get away from company and think things out, Eric would take himself off to one of his havens, and just rest there, often taking a small stock of food so that he need not leave his hiding place for days on end. He knew that Bonnet would be able to find him if anything happened, as she knew roughly where each of his hidden homes was; but it was the best way to put his thoughts in order and decide what to do next. Having retrieved Bonnet, there was no need for him to stay at Hackney Mansions any longer, so when that clear, fresh morning dawned, he was up early and ready to leave before the rest of them awoke.

Thickpea, on the other hand, wanted to stay on a bit. It was always a wrench to leave Eric, but from time to time she needed to be a rat again, and this was a good time to take advantage of being in the right place and not be required by her beloved Eric. So as he packed up his few belongings in his bag, she sat and watched, cleaning herself and snuffling quietly. He did not need telling. He stared at her for a moment, then smiled.

"Okay," he said, "only behave yourself. I'll see you soon."

In the time away from Eric, Thickpea remained with the other rats that inhabited the old school, exploring the buildings and the grounds, learning the runs and feeding spots in neighbouring gardens, and catching up on relationships with her own kind. She did not eat as well as usual, and her bed was nowhere near Eric's pocket in terms of comfort; but it would not do to lose her skills to survive without Eric. She scavenged and scampered, fled the pest controller as he patrolled the streets, stole scraps of food from under kitchen tables in the houses, sat on an upstairs window sill admiring the sunsets over the chimneys and rooftops with their adornment of television aerials and large, round dishes that capture the pictures from above the clouds. She never understood all those human things, but she know the basics from eavesdropping on conversations between men and women sitting in their living rooms as they watched the moving pictures.

Thickpea learned so much from time spent watching people as they went about their lives at Hackney Mansions.

Winnie, Old Yar and Bonnet stayed there together for a time; this was one of Winnie's and Old Yar's main homes, and Bonnet was persuaded to stay for her own safety and for the comfort of having company after her harrowing experience. The morning that Eric left had been quiet, as they realised that he needed his own company more than theirs, so each of them went about their tasks as normal but subdued. Then on one of his regular rummages around the school, Old Yar found a box full of old school books in the cellar, and he and Bonnet spent a merry time looking through them. The old sailor found an old atlas, which kept him occupied for hours, checking out the old trade routes across the oceans, and counting off the countries he had visited as he turned the pages. Then as the day drew to a close, he closed the atlas with a snap, making Bonnet jump, and lifted his lean frame out of the chair with a groan.

"Time for my yarn with the old hands down at the Green," he said, and off he went to meet his cronies for their nightly chinwag and gossip. They would sit on the benches on Hackney Downs and sup from bottles in brown paper bags, exchanging news and reminiscing about past lives. The hours would pass quickly enough, then some would bed themselves down on the benches, some would wander back to their own havens and slumber out of sight, and Old Yar would straighten his beard, stand with a groan and make for Hackney Mansions. It was not often that he offered a bed to any of the other under-worlders—they each appreciated having their own little worlds to go back to—but that night was an exception. After a long, serious talk with the other vagrants, it was the early hours of the morning when Old Yar rolled up back home, with another old man in tow, and a mission to complete. He had heard disturbing news.

Winnie had disappeared for most of the day, returning just before dark with a bag full of something that smelled rather musty. She emptied it out on a tabletop and rooted through the contents, um-ing and ah-ing at each item.

"That's an old shawl, I think, with lots of lace and a huge fringe across the bottom. It's so not me, don't you think! And there's not much money in that these days, I'm afraid. Oh, here's a lovely blouse, always been one of my favourite colours, this shade of peach. See, how do I look? Cool? Wuw!"

Bonnet looked up from the book she was reading, a pair of glasses perched on the end of her nose.

"Oh yes, it's very, er, cool," she said appreciatively. "Where did you find them?"

"In a bag left outside a charity shop," Winnie explained. "They put a notice on the door telling people not to leave stuff outside, but it doesn't stop them, and as it gives us a chance to forage for ourselves, I'm not complaining. Makes me feel, like, rather clever, really."

Winnie giggled like a young girl and carried on her rummaging.

"I just hope they weren't worn by anybody with anything fictitious."

Bonnet looked at her, puzzled.

"Fictitious? You mean infectious?"

"That's what I said, dear. Ooh, there's a lovely thick sock here. What are the chances of finding its pair ... yay, *there* we go—Old Yar will make good use of these over the winter. Have you seen his child's brains? Some mornings he can hardly walk, his toes are so painful. I keep telling him to see a doctor, or a chiro-, chiro-, oh I don't know what they're called, but he says it's a question of self-respect, going to a charity surgery. A load of nonsense, I think, but he can't help his pride. I would have thought his feet were more important than his dignity. And there's a couple of jumpers that'll fit you, dear, or maybe Eric would like the dark blue one if it's his size. What do you think?"

"Mmm," was the only reply Bonnet could muster, still deep in her book.

Winnie smiled.

"What are you reading, dear?"

Bonnet put the book down, and pushed the glasses even closer to the end of her nose so that she peered over the top of them.

"'Day of the Triffids', it's called," she said, reading from the cover, "science fiction, with some poor syntax but a great story."

"Poor what?" Winnie looked puzzled.

"Syntax. You know, use of language. Correct English, punctuation, that sort of thing. So important, or so my old friend Charles Dickens told me the other day."

"You must stop telling these porkies, like, dear," chided Winnie, smoothing out her new clothes and laying them flat on the table. "You know perfectly well that Charles Dickens died years ago."

"In 1870, to be exact," replied Bonnet, pushing her glasses back to their proper place and picking up the book ready to continue reading. "But that doesn't mean I can't talk to him. He just popped over from the other side for a chat and a change of scenery." With that, she bent forward and lifted the book to her face, marking the end of the conversation. Winnie picked up the dark blue jumper and put it to one side, ready to give to Eric when he returned.

Four Days to Christmas

The following morning, after a night spent scavenging in the nearby gardens with her old friends and a handful of new ones, Thickpea returned to the skirting board in the staff room for a nap. Bonnet had bedded down in a classroom along the corridor, having manoeuvred a pair of bookshelves to make two walls of a small makeshift bedroom, lined with any old rags she had accumulated, and with her hat bag in pride of place on one of the shelves. Winnie was usually the first to rise, with her busy, motherly need to tidy the furniture, wipe the tabletop and get the staff room ready for the day; then Bonnet would yawn and stretch her way into the room, wearing whichever hat she chose to set the tone for the day. Old Yar, sleeping upstairs in his broom cupboard, took his time waking up. "Old sea dogs never lie in," he had told Eric, "but you can't hurry the tide, lad." Winnie said it was because of his nights out with the cronies where he would share some drinks as well as stories, to help him sleep—but not today. He was down at first light and went into the cloakroom to wake Winnie with a good, hard shake.

Winnie sat up, still half dazed with sleep, and tried to move quickly but nearly fell onto the floor.

"Hey, dude, what are you doing? Is something up?"

Thickpea was standing by the open door, having spent a pleasant night out scavenging with her mates, returning to hear Old Yar blundering around in his noisy way. He looked even more untidy than usual, with the straggly beard not even combed with his fingers, as was always part of his daily routine to keep himself as presentable as possible. His face was drawn and haggard, as if he needed another few hours of sleep, but something was bothering him.

"Last night, my old storm petrel, I heard things. You need to know," he spoke urgently, pulling Winnie to her feet quite gently but firmly. "The boy—he's in trouble."

11

Bad News Man

Winnie stood up and made her way to a window. There she found a tiny shard of glass, and moved it from side to side until it reflected the light and she could use it as a mirror to look at her face, pull her hair into some semblance of order, and rub the sleep from her eyes.

"What do you mean?" She did not seem concerned. Perhaps she had not caught the touch of fear that Thickpea had detected in what Old Yar had said.

"It's Eric, you deaf old buzzard, he's in a bother. Have you seen him over the last few days? I know he's not been here, but maybe you saw him when you were out yesterday."

"No, I don't think so," said Winnie, frowning as she tried to remember. "Should I have done, like?"

"Well, it would be better for him if you had. The police are looking for a lad who matches Eric's description. They say he was involved in kidnapping that young lass, you know, the one Belt was after rescuing."

Winnie turned to stare at him.

"What? Belt? He's set Eric up?"

Old Yar moved to a chair and sat down heavily.

"I don't know. It sounds as though the police had an anonymous phone call, telling them to go to that house in Pickering Avenue where the boy found Bonnet—"

"But Eric said he left the kidnapper there, all wrapped up."

"Well, he wasn't there any more. Remember, he said something about a van coming as they left? That would have been an accomplice. It sounds as though they cleared out of there, but not before leaving just enough clues to incriminate our Eric."

"What sort of clues?"

"Well, my source tells me they found a gold ring on the floor in the hall."

Winnie gasped.

"But he so doesn't have that. You said he doesn't even know about that."

"I know. He doesn't. We always swore he never would, and as long as he didn't know he would be safe here. So—that means somebody left it there to point the finger at him. If they start to piece the bits of the yarn together, they'll end up looking for him."

"But it must have been one of us. Who knows? Who would do that to him?"

Old Yar just shook his head.

"And how did you hear about it?"

Old Yar paused, then spoke more slowly.

"Well, actually, I've brought him here, to stay for a while, you know, keep out of sight, hiding in a sea fret, as it were, just in case word gets out he's been talking, if you see what I mean."

He coughed loudly and obviously, and a figure appeared in the doorway. Winnie managed to stop herself gasping in horror at the sight that met her eyes. This was a man she would not have chosen as a companion. Nobody would have. Not with a scarred face like that. He would attract far too much attention.

The man moved forward with a severe limp. His body was lopsided, the left shoulder hanging low and the right hand curled round, held tight against his chest. Long, greasy hair hid some of his features, but nothing could completely cover a bright red scar that flashed across his face, from his left cheek over his nose to his right temple. The scar weeped, leaving trickles of blood down the side of his nose and round his dribbling mouth. This was a sad creature, living with such unsightly disfigurements—but his eyes were a startling blue and as clear and honest as Winnie had ever seen. Her horror instantly turned to a mixture of pity, admiration and guilt at her own reaction. She stood up, moving towards him and holding out her hand.

"Welcome to Hackney Mansions, like," she said softly. "I'm Winnie. Good to make your acquaintance, or whatever. What does it mean, whatever? I only say it 'cos the youngsters do today. And you are?"

The man took a step backwards, then held out his hand in return.

"Newton, at you service," he replied. It was a quiet voice, cracked as if dragged across broken glass, but with a gentleness that Winnie read as being trustworthy. This one was true, she thought. Mind you, she reminded herself, she had said that of Belt. Now she was not so sure.

Old Yar motioned to a chair and the three of them sank into soggy armchairs.

"Tell Winnie what you told me—"

"Tell us both."

Bonnet was standing in the doorway, a look of deep concern on her face.

"I heard what you said earlier. So get on with it. What's the story?"

She sat on the floor, curled up by Winnie's feet, and nobody thought to remark that their Hat Girl was not wearing any disguise at all. She had come as herself.

Newton looked at each of them in turn, then began.

"I had been attacked. This scar—I was in the wrong place at the wrong time. It's not relevant, so I won't bore you with details. But I was at the police station filling out a witness statement when there was a big fuss and a young constable came in. He whispered to my policeman, who had just finished writing up my version of the assault, but didn't whisper quietly enough. An anonymous phone call had led the police to a house, where they were told they would find out more about the abduction of the young girl. The officer said the ring they found at the house had been identified as one taken from the body of a car accident victim four years ago near Alexandra Palace, when a woman was killed, a man severely injured, but a boy who was in the car must have wandered off and was never found. The wedding ring, bearing the inscription Joanna and Tom Dyson 1987, was a plain band of gold with a twisted rope effect round it, very distinctive. The husband, who ended up in hospital, wore a matching one, so it was easy to identify. It was found on the floor of the hallway of 27 Pickering Avenue, and upstairs were signs of there having been two people living in the rooms. DNA testing showed one of them to be Ellie Bagnall, the young girl abducted a few days ago. Her father has been missing for days, and there's a theory that he had taken Ellie abroad. The other DNA was female, but they don't know who."

Bonnet said nothing. Both Winnie and Old Yar looked at her, but decided to keep quiet. Newton continued.

"So the police are searching for Bagnall, with his daughter, as well as the Dyson boy who walked away from the fatal crash four years ago. They reckon he holds the answers to this mystery. They're setting up a full-scale search for him, fearing he'll abduct another young girl, possibly for ransom."

"So that's what's it's about," muttered Bonnet. She did not know about Eric's past, but now things seemed to make sense. He had been there about four years, almost as long as she herself had. He had no recollection of his life before arriving at the Mansions late one Sunday evening, with blood on his clothes but unhurt. He had slept for two days and nights, then just got up and started his new life. Bonnet had always thought there was something in Eric's mind that was blotting out something painful in his past. Now she knew what it was. The boy was being set up.

12

Gravestone Haven

"We need to warn the boy," Old Yar decided. "And at full speed. Does anybody know where he is?"

"I do. But before I go—"

Bonnet turned to Newton.

"Your scar. You say it's not connected with this, but—how did you get it?"

Newton squirmed uncomfortably.

"I was standing in a crowd of like-minded folk, in a protest against animal testing, outside a company building in the city. They've been using innocent animals to test for chemical reactions, and we'd heard rumours they were even experimenting with them, giving them nerve gases or drugs to change their characters, or give them special abilities. All sounded very science fiction, but the guy I was with was convinced the hearsay was reliable. Well, a big fat slob of a man came over to us and tried to push us out of the way. He said they needed to clear the area for a fire alarm test, and we needed to leave, now. Some of the crowd took exception to this, and pushed back. Well, I'm not a tall guy, so I got stuck in the middle, and things turned nasty. The greasy bloke pulled out a knife and started flashing it around wildly. I got in the way. That's all there is to it, really."

The three listeners stared open-mouthed. Old Yar was the first to react.

"That is dreadful. Criminal. Were the police called?"

Newton smiled wryly.

"Not until too late. The crowd had largely dispersed by then, not wanting to get involved, and I was ushered inside the building and an ambulance was called. The few that stayed with me, including my mate, kicked up a fuss, of course, but the company boss came down and started throwing ten pound notes around like confetti, and that did the trick. No more story."

"What about your attacker? Did he get his come-uppance?"

"Last thing I heard, from my mate, he'd been sacked, for over-reacting. He's not been seen again, and nobody's dared to picket the building since. So now, somewhere out there on the streets, is a very dangerous guy on the loose, without a job, possibly with a grudge against the firm for sacking him, and with me, for being in the wrong place at the wrong time."

"Give me his name," Old Yar said, reaching for a scrap of paper to write it down, "I'll put out the word to watch for him."

"His name," Newton almost spat the words out, "is Sprockett."

Thickpea's blood ran cold.

Bonnet scrabbled to her feet, grabbed a hat from her bag, picked up a small green rucksack, then sped off through the door. As she walked quickly away, she pushed her hair behind her ears and pulled an army cap onto her head, altering her appearance considerably. She now looked smart, and walked with a straight back and a firm, confident stride of a person who had a mission to complete. It took Thickpea a moment to come to her senses, but it made sense for her to follow; she scampered after Bonnet, catching up when she crossed the Downs Road and jumping into her rucksack without her noticing. She was too intent on reaching Eric before anybody official found him.

They made their way to the railway, to follow the usual routes taken by all underworlders—picking their way through the dead grass, the bits of food packing thrown from the train windows, the old bedsteads and shopping trolleys abandoned on the embankments. After a while Bonnet decided it was easier to walk along the track itself. It meant she had to keep her ears open for any trains coming, to give her time to leap aside but the going was easier and faster. The trains rumbled past every twenty minutes or so, and it made the journey rather disjointed as she flung herself face down into the debris, then dusted herself off, straightened her army cap and carried on.

Just before reaching Stoke Newington Station, Bonnet left the railway track and made for the cemetery that lay just beyond the fire station, where she was sure Eric would have found the peace he craved. She was still walking fast, skirting the lands used to train the fire fighters with their hoses and wonderful hats—she longed to own one of those—and found a gap in the perimeter wall of the cemetery, creeping through and heading for the central area of plots where the oldest, most neglected graves were. Here was where Eric had made his haven, but she was not sure of its exact position, and finding it was a task to be undertaken carefully. She would not hurt Eric's feelings for anything, especially after he had saved her from her captor, and giving away his precious haven would spoil their friendship beyond measure.

But this was where Thickpea came in. She did know. She squeaked from her hiding place in the rucksack, causing Bonnet to yelp and turn round, expecting to see something on the ground behind her. The rat jumped down and ran towards a tall statue of an angel holding a book. There she stopped, squeaked again, and hoped the lass would not take fright and run away.

Bonnet turned and looked at Thickpea. The rat stood her ground and snuffled, washed her whiskers, and tried to beckon her on. It took a few minutes for the girl to understand, but somehow she decided, and she moved forwards. Thickpea moved on, passing the book-reading angel and making for a tomb with an ugly obelisk marked with strange scratches, along an unmown path of grass alongside several graves surrounded with iron railings, then on to a pile of tumbled-down headstones where she knew Eric would be—if he was 'at home'. She kept glancing over her shoulder to make sure Bonnet was following; she was, her eyes wide and wondering. She had no idea that Eric had a rat for a companion.

They found the right clump of brambles and ran through them, taking care not to get too scratched, but failing. Beneath a gravestone that lay horizontally on four short pillars, Thickpea found Eric, nestling for warmth under a sheet of plastic covered by a thick layer of turf. In her excitement she squeaked loudly, making him jump. He looked at her with a worried expression; his friend's unexpected appearance couldn't mean good news.

"Thickpea?"

He crawled out of his bed, edging round the brambles, and came face to face with Bonnet.

"There you are, old chap!" she barked. "Look lively there, we've trouble ahead. Message from the top, been to a war council back at HQ. Your cover is blown, captain. You are a marked man."

Eric had not followed any of this and looked bewildered, his eyes passing from Bonnet to Thickpea and back again as he tried to take it all in.

"What?"

"Don't you salute a senior officer in your regiment, sonny?" Bonnet pulled herself up to her full height—this did not take long—as she pursed her lips.

"Oh, yes, sorry, sir," Eric touched his forehead with his fingers.

"Well, if that's the best you can do … come on, we must get out of view. You're on the wanted list at the local cop shop."

Eric blinked a few times, getting his thoughts in order, then grabbed Bonnet by the arm, dragging her into the brambles beyond the gravestone bed and behind a tall obelisk, where he had made a flat area in the middle of the long grass, and manufactured a larger roof with another piece of plastic. There they sat while Thickpea ran up and down the boy's chest, making sure he was okay, then heading back to her pocket where she could eavesdrop in comfort.

Bonnet took a deep breath, and frowned. She removed her hat, reverting to herself to tell the tale. This had never happened before, as far as Eric knew. It must be serious.

"Listen carefully, Eric. It concerns your past, the part of your past you can't remember. There was a car crash near Alexandra Palace—"

The story unfolded slowly, Bonnet telling with care and precision. She related how the woman had died, the father left seriously injured and taken to hospital, the boy fleeing from the scene; the anonymous call to the police leading them to 27 Pickering Avenue and the finding of the ring with Joanna and Tom Dyson's inscription on it; Eric's name on a list of wanted people. Eric sat in front of her, hugging his knees, his face down, contemplating his thin, cold shoes.

"How did Old Yar find all this out? I mean, did he know already?"

"He and Winnie were talking as though it was old news. A man called Newton, with a hideous scar on his face, came back to tell us himself what he had heard at the cop shop. I didn't know him, or anything about it before. And if you like, nobody will ever hear it from me."

Bonnet got up quietly and moved away. Thickpea was burrowing frantically in Eric's pocket, searching for crumbs, but she seemed to know he needed to be alone for a while.

So that was it. That was what had happened. The truth had come back in a flash as clear and sharp as a blade. It had been all his fault. The accident that had killed his mother, that had left his father in hospital, probably dead by now, that had caused him to run away from the reality he had caused. Eric, the selfish, arrogant, obnoxious young boy who always wanted for himself, demanding until he worked himself into a tantrum, screaming for—whatever he could think of, maybe a new mountain bike, or a computer game, or just an ice cream. Usually it worked, but recently his father was beginning to be more stubborn, refusing the boy's demands for newer, bigger, better. That day, it had been a pair of expensive football boots. His best friend—who was called, what was it now, Simon, that's it—had been bought a lovely pair for his birthday the week before, and Eric wanted some that cost more, to show off his power over gullible and weak parents and keep his status in the classroom. Father had said no. Mother had tried to calm them down. Eric shouted, pleaded, wept, thumped the back of his father's car seat, sulked, then shouted again. A sudden bellow had caused his dad to turn the wheel with unexpected ferocity, the car slamming into the kerb and hurling them all forward. What followed was still hazy, but Eric remembered running away from the car as it smouldered, its front pushed in by the impact with the ancient tree stump. He turned back just once. Nothing moved inside the car. He was sure his parents must be dead.

The guilt swept over Eric like a hot, glowing wave, so that every pore of his body burned with shame, his cheeks flushed crimson, his breath catching in his tightened throat. This was what his mind had managed to blank out for four years. He had caused a death. He had killed his mother, and, maybe, his father too. A wealth of memories of his childhood swamped his brain—playing in a large grassy garden, kicking a football into a goal mouth where his father stood, running back to a smiling mother who was carrying a tray of cakes and drinks for them all; snuggled on a sofa in front of an open fire, reading a comic, tucking into a gooey chocolate bar; walking to school with a handful of friends, all chatting and joking, laughter ringing in his ears; lying in a huge bed next to his mother on a dark night with the thunder and lightning crashing about outside. Each snippet of memory emerged with a warm glow as it materialised in his mind, but vanished with a pop to leave a cold, emptiness behind.

Eric didn't realise it, but every emotion he felt touched Thickpea too. She was so close to him, cuddling the front of his jacket where his tummy was, that each tiny pinprick of feeling reached her. The love, the pain, the distress, the cold self-hate that was building up inside him—she reacted to them all. Her confusion from this burst of different sensations made her nuzzle even closer, anxious for her beloved Eric and for herself.

Bonnet stood back, away from the hideout so as not to draw any attention to it if somebody saw her there. She paced along the path, she examined the wild flowers, she read the names on the gravestones, but always keeping half an eye turned back towards Eric, so she was ready to return to him when he called.

After what seemed like an age, he rose from his haven, stretching himself and looking around as if seeking something he did not expect to find. Maybe, Bonnet thought, he hoped it was a dream, that he would wake up back in Hackney Mansions, where the only worries were Winnie's asteroids and Old Yar's child's brains. She watched as he turned and scanned the cemetery, his gaze eventually falling on her.

"Okay?" she asked tentatively.

"No," he replied shortly, "not yet, anyway."

Thickpea poked her head out of his grasp. Bonnet stared at her.

"I see you've met," remarked Eric calmly.

"Mmm, well, not formally introduced," she retorted. "I await that with great joy."

Eric smiled, a rather stiff smile but it was better than nothing. He began to pace up and down between the gravestones, careful not to tread on the souls of those who had been keeping him company every night. When he spoke again, it was with a firmness and decision that surprised Bonnet after all he had had to digest.

"I will stay here for a bit longer, but not for ever. I want to make for the hostel at Christmas, I'm not missing that. How many days is it to Christmas?"

Bonnet smirked. "What are you asking me for?"

"Oh, I just wondered ... Still, tell Old Yar I'll see him there. I need to think things through. You'd better head back."

Bonnet nodded, pulled her army cap out of her bag, slipped it on, touched its rim like in a salute, and made her way out of the haven. She left alone, Thickpea deciding to stay with Eric; and he was glad of her company.

13

Thinking Time

Three Days to Christmas

Eric was woken next morning by a strange sensation. Thickpea seemed to be trying to burrow into his chest. She was nibbling at his clothing and scrabbling furiously with her front paws in an attempt to get away from something. He put his hands around her, lifting her away from him and trying to keep her still. Her wriggling made it difficult to focus on her tiny face and calm her down.

"Hey! Give it up, will you? You're okay, you daft—"

Then he froze. Outside, a twig cracked. There was somebody out there. As if she knew what was best, Thickpea froze too. All four ears underneath the gravestone were tuned in to any out-of-the-ordinary sounds. Sure enough, another twig betrayed a presence. Then, a swishing of hands through grass, as though somebody was searching. Eric shivered. There was no reason for anybody to be there—unless they were looking for him. They remained stock-still, hardly daring to breath as the rhythmic rustling and crackling passed them by. Whoever it was, they were being very thorough. Eric prayed that he had left no signs of occupation.

After a while, the swooshing began to fade. The searcher was moving away. Eric waited until it had almost disappeared altogether before moving, gently putting down the bundle of shaking fur that had been barely breathing in his grasp all that time, and slowly edging to the entrance of the haven. He glanced over the gravestone and looked over the ranks of headstones. In the distance was Blondie. He concentrated on the ground by his feet, still searching intently for anything that would betray Eric's presence. Eric watched, Thickpea beside him on the granite top, until the young man moved out of sight behind a distant row of graves. They were alone again; but Eric's most peaceful site had been invaded.

The two of them stayed at the cemetery, spending the short, dark days foraging and thinking, or clearing the patch of all life signs and thinking. During the long, cold nights they remained snuggled together—while thinking—in their makeshift home of cardboard and blankets. The simplicity of their days kept them occupied, with the basic needs uppermost in their minds and no complications to clutter up the hours. From time to time Eric took himself off, walking through the graveyard, thinking hard. Bonnet had promised to return in a few days to report on the latest news, but until then they remained in a blissful ignorance of what was happening in the big wide world.

Every morning Thickpea would be awakened by Eric's slow, sluggish movements as the pangs of hunger woke him from his sleep. They would raid their limited stores of food, scavenged whenever and wherever they could from the dustbins of the houses around the edge of the graveyard. Meals would consist of the remains of pizza boxes still lined with congealed cheese and bits of doughy bread, followed by half-eaten satsumas; and one day they made their way along a particularly wide road with vast houses that Eric said looked like mini palaces, and found the remains of a tray of smoked salmon, with several bowls of soggy white stuff Eric called dips, and some sticks of hard, crunchy bread. That, Eric informed Thickpea, was a banquet, and they rummaged deeper in the recycling boxes until they found half a bottle of wine to accompany it. That night Eric even lit a candle stump and put a rag on the floor for a tablecloth, so they could eat in style.

So food was not a problem, leaving time to spare for long walks to the reservoirs, where they would watch the ducks and coots scudding across the water and throw stones at any floating debris, to try and make it sink out of sight. Once they were chased by Kal and the Fractured Jawbone gang,—making the most of the school holidays during the last days before Christmas. They shouted at Eric, calling him Crash Boy and Loser, then tossed rotten fruit at them, but he wasn't worried. Eric knew that land so well that he always had the means to escape, and he was sure they would never find the gravestone haven. He just ran out of sight, then slowed to walking pace and continued on his way when the gang lost interest in him, so they could wander from street to street, comparing the Christmas lights hanging outside the houses, and laughing at the dreadful decorations some people put on their front doors

Bonnet arrived the following morning, soon after the day dawned. It was still quite dark, with thick cloud promising rain later, and she wore a see-through rainhood over her long hair. The maid approached with a slightly bent back, holding the base of her spine with her hand, and grimacing.

"Dear me, this damp weather is not doing my old bones any good," she groaned as she made herself comfortable on a pile of blankets. "The doctor told me it was half-ritis, but I don't believe a word of it. This pain must be something much more serious, I know, I can feel it in my water."

"But there is news, young man," she continued, pulling a pair of knitting needles attached to a ball of wool and proceeding to knit. "Belt has been back to Hackney Mansions."

"Belt came back? But what for?"

"To find out what else he could about the rescue and anybody involved, as he was planning to tell the police everything he could to clear your name."

Eric took a deep breath.

"You mean—I'm in the clear?"

"Exactly that, my boy. The police have now issued an e-fit photo of a young blond man they want to find—"

"Blond? Did you say blond?" Eric sat up, taking great interest now.

"Yes, dear, blond, didn't you hear me? Have you ever thought of having your ears syringed? Well, it seems that Belt has set them on the trail of your Blondie and the dirty white van that carried me to that dreadful house."

"But what about the ring? I thought I was supposed to have stolen that from the car after the accident?"

"Well, Belt managed to persuade the police to leave that bit of the detecting with him. Turns out, he's working in insurance, you see. I'm thinking of asking him for a job, actually. Could be just up my street." She clattered the knitting needles briskly, then said sharply, "Damn! Dropped a stitch."

So at least Eric could get to the Christmas hostel without fear of being apprehended as a felon. The future was brighter, but there were still questions to answer.

"When are you all making your way to the hostel?" he asked.

Bonnet clicked away with her knitting. "Very soon, Old Yar said. He wants to be sure of a good bed in the dormitory, not one on the end of the row nearest to the smelly toilets."

"Okay, then I'll meet you there," Eric decided, "and I suppose I'll have to face the police some time. Better sooner than later. At least Adrian and Jess at the hostel will back me up, if they're still there, that is."

So it was decided. Bonnet returned to Hackney Mansions with the news that Eric was well and would see them all at the hostel the following Saturday. He and Thickpea sat late into the night, planning their route down into the city. The rat felt his excitement as a warm glow, starting in her toes and slowly filtering up until her nose felt it was glowing red. As they gathered their few travelling belongings, they both found it hard to stay calm.

14

A Wobbly Ride

Two Days to Christmas

In the unpleasantly chilly days leading up to Christmas, the journey taken by hundreds of street dwellers through the streets of north London as they headed for a few days of sanctuary went largely unnoticed. They were just the homeless, on the move as usual. People to be ignored, despised, even hated for their not belonging to the normal human race. They needed a wash, shouldn't clutter up the streets, must get a job and start to pay their way in society again. Well, sometimes life just isn't that straightforward.

Every one of Eric's friends and acquaintances had a story to tell, and every story was different. He himself had run from a situation he couldn't cope with—a death, an accident, a life of guilt and trying to live with shame. Old Yar had lost his line of work on the seas when he became too old for the hard labour involved, and had no other home to go to, preferring the open air blowing through his beard to the dry, stale atmosphere hemmed in by roof and walls. Doldrum, Eric's first vagrant companion, had made her way onto the streets to escape a violent husband and a miserable existence. Winnie, always vague about her background and reluctant to discuss her past, hinted at medical problems, with a childhood blighted by bouts of drooping cough and weasles, as she charmingly put it. The variety of reasons for being homeless must be as long as the number of people on the streets. Perhaps this means that any help that would ease them back into normal life must be as varied and flexible as possible, as every solution will be unique too. Eric had come to realise the complexity of the problem in his four vagrant years, and had developed a solemn respect for all the poor souls whose lifestyle he now shared.

He began his long trek into the city on a Sunday morning, under a grey sky that threatened snow. Thickpea was snuggled in his usual pocket, staring through the torn seam at the sights being pointed out surreptitiously by Eric as they walked. It was an uneventful journey on the whole, apart from one scary moment when Thickpea peeped out and found herself face to face with a young child who was staring rudely at Eric. There was a loud scream as the child ran away towards his mother, yelling that he had seen a rat; but his mother simply shushed and scolded the boy, telling him not to be rude about poor unfortunate people who don't have homes of their own. The rat made sure to keep out of sight from then on.

They followed the railway line, as that was the method Eric was most familiar with; keeping as close as he could to the actual route of the trains and resorting to walking along the track itself when the public roads moved too far away. That way he did not get lost, and Thickpea had the chance to see others of her species and make new friends of her own. They followed the line from Stoke Newington station, with its high walls keeping it hidden from the view of the local shoppers, and passed Rectory Road and Hackney Down stations before they stopped for a bite of lunch. Then they cut across Graham Road towards London Fields, where they played at being explorers as they hacked their way through the thick undergrowth of brambles and tree roots. As they emerged from the south side, still breathless and Eric wearing a huge grin, they pulled up short. There in front of them was Blondie, walking nonchalantly along Lansdowne Drive past the school, arms swinging casually and head held high. He was heading away from them, but it was definitely him, and Eric reacted immediately.

"Hey!"

Blondie turned, a look of alarm spreading over his face, a look Thickpea felt as a shiver travelled up from her tail to her whiskers. Then he was off, racing away up the road, away from the railway where Eric felt most comfortable and into the muddle of streets with tidy gardens and multi-coloured garage doors, past the swimming pool, then down towards Bethnal Green. Eric gave chase, his few belongings wobbling and rattling in the shoulder bag as he galloped after his prey. Thickpea felt very unsafe, and held on to the material of the pocket with her teeth to make sure she didn't fall out.

Blondie was fast. He headed back towards the railway for a while, then made for a cul-de-sac behind a museum, not far from a police station; that might be handy, Eric noted.

"Let's hang back," spluttered Eric breathlessly, "let him think he's lost us."

He slowed, letting his quarry get out of sight as he entered the cul-de-sac, and watched from the shelter of a thick privet hedge. Blondie ran to the front door of one of the houses, glanced behind him and scanned the area, then knocked, opened it and entered without waiting for a reply.

"Your turn, Thickpea," Eric coaxed her out of her hiding place, almost pulling her teeth out as she was still clamped tightly onto the pocket. "Go in there, check it out, and come back here; I'll know if you're okay."

The rat shook herself, checked all her teeth were intact, then scampered after Blondie.

The door had closed by the time she reached it, but she found a window that was slightly open and managed to squeeze through. She scurried up to the next doorway, and listened. Beyond the threshold were two men talking. She poked her tiny head round the edge of the door, but there was no way she could enter. The floor was clear, there was nothing to hide behind, and she would have been spotted as soon as she ventured into the room. She had to be content with just listening.

"That was stupid. What were you thinking of, coming here, you foolish, brainless oaf?"

"I had no choice. The boy saw me. He ran after me, but I lost him way back, he's not a chance of finding us here. And don't call me brainless. You're not perfect yourself, you know."

"I'm glad you're so sure of yourself. After the mess you made of keeping the girl safe—you are such an idiot. Heaven only knows what your mum'll say about all this."

"Oh, stop trying to put me down. I've done just as well as anybody else in this caper, haven't I? It's not easy, trying to live up to my family's expectations."

The other man guffawed.

"Your family's expectation? That sounds as if you are expecting to profit from this as much as those who thought it out in the first place. Watch yourself, brainless. You're not indispensable. I can deal with you any time I want."

"What do you mean? Hey, what are you making like a gorilla for? Not that you need to try hard—stop doing that. Let go of me—"

There was a scuffling, the sound of two men grappling, and suddenly the splintering of glass, and a loud scream. It seemed like a good time to get away from the door, and Thickpea dashed back outside. Something thumped heavily in the garden to the side of the house, and she heard footsteps as Sprockett lumbered down the stairs and out of the house. Thickpea heard a car start up and drive away, and only then did she venture out to see what had happened.

Blondie was lying in a crumpled heap in a patch of shrubs, his watery eyes closed, the long nose streaked with blood. He lay very still and his left leg was stretched out at an unusual angle. She approached gingerly and sniffed his face. He was breathing, but quite unconscious. She ran back to the front gate, and squealed. It was her sign to Eric that he was needed, and he appeared without delay. Running up to the fallen figure in the bushes, he was soon joined by a handful of the neighbours—Thickpea's signal to hide from view—all making "Oooh!" and Oh how awful" noises, and one of them went home to ring for an ambulance. While everybody was occupied, Thickpea decided to return inside the house. It was a good opportunity to do a bit of snooping of her own.

The inner room was cold now as the door had been left open and the winter chill had taken hold. There was a musty smell, which is rather nice to a rat, and not much litter lying around to scavenge through. But underneath a thickly padded sofa she caught a glimpse of something shiny. It was a tiny gold charm, in the shape of a football boot, attached to a fine gold chain. Not without difficulty Thickpea picked it up, and sped back to Eric. She could hear the approaching siren of the ambulance and knew he would want to be away from there before it arrived.

She was not sure why, but Thickpea did not show Eric the football boot charm and chain she found in the house. She sneaked in into her pocket and managed to nestle it in the folds of material near the seam, but not too close to the torn bit. It was important, she knew that much, but did not know what role it had to play in this mystery.

15

Teabreak

Holly Christmas Hostel was one of several set up in London over the festive season. They were all situated in derelict office blocks, where kind businessmen had allowed the charity to take over their property for a short while to give some Christmas cheer to those who otherwise wouldn't get any. Holly Hostel was close to the business district by Liverpool Street Station, close to some of the most up-to-date architectural marvels the city had to offer, which made its scruffy exterior stand out even more. Its entrance was an unassuming doorway, up a set of steps and with a revolving door that complained with a loud squeak whenever it was put into use. The glass on the doors was as grubby as that in the windows; when the lamps were switched on inside the large reception rooms, hardly any light escaped out onto the street, the glass was so grimy. But the days before Christmas saw a steady stream of people entering, every one weary, footsore and in need of a shower and a hearty meal.

A young man spent the day standing just inside the revolving door, welcoming every newcomer. His name was Adrian, and he wore jeans and a baggy t-shirt bearing the slogan 'Loudon Offkey III, Music to Curl your Toes', and he had been volunteering at the hostel for three years now, so he was known by many of the homeless who were about to arrive. A friendly, known face was always a welcome sight. His slender frame was topped off with a ponytail and several earrings, not all of them through his ears, and his pale face was covered in pimples and thick dollops of spot lotion. The impression he gave was not good, suggesting a person with nothing better to do than stand there, but when he smiled at each new arrival, his gawky demeanour vanished. His smile came from within, its friendly light shining out with a goodwill that softened the toughest vagrant and helped them to accept the charity that was offered at the festive season.

Eric and Thickpea arrived late in the day, the sky dark and threatening to douse them in soggy half-snow half-rain. The streets were wet, and the traffic thundered by as the working population made their noisy, bad-tempered way home.

As they stood outside the hostel looking up at the filthy windows and not feeling too optimistic about the next few days in a place so grimy, a small blue van pulled up beside them. The passenger window wound down and the beaming face of Mrs Burgonya greeted Eric.

"Eric! Good to see, good to see," she crooned, holding her hands cupped together and bobbing them up and down as if shaking something, "I wish to speak, have you some time?"

Eric smiled back though surprised by her sudden appearance.

"Hello, Mrs Burgonya, Mr Burgonya." He leaned down and saw the tall redheaded beanpole of a man in the driving seat. "Who is looking after the shop?"

"No open today, Eric, is Sunday!" he bellowed over his wife, who was still beaming and bobbing her hands. "We bring food for the hostel, we make our donation."

"Ah, I see." Eric understood now. The shopkeepers throughout London will have been asked to support the Christmas hostels by providing goods to last them over the festive period, and this was the Burgonya's contribution. They were a good family, and it was his way of repaying the help Mr Burgonya received from Old Yar and his cronies when he was homeless too.

"You say you need to speak to me?"

Mrs Burgonya suddenly stopped beaming and looked serious.

"Yes, it is important. You need to know," she urged, and beckoned to him.

Eric looked longingly up at the dirty window, and sighed. A comfy bed would have to wait a bit longer. He reached down, opened the van door and squeezed in beside Mrs Burgonya. Not an easy task for it was a very small van.

Mr Burgonya did not drive far. He took them round the back streets until they reached a tiny café with a picture of a coffee bean suspended over the front door. He pulled into a parking slot close by, wedging the van between a Mercedes and a Lexus, and then shepherded them into the café. There, once settled with a large mug of tea and a toasted teacake, Mrs Burgonya began to talk.

"Eric, Old Yar, he visit us the other day—he say you now know who you are. Your surname is Dyson, your mother died in a car crash, your father was injured, you ran from the accident, that you already know. But there is more."

Eric gulped a huge mouthful of hot tea and nearly burned his mouth, coughing and spluttering. Mr Burgonya patted him heartily on the back and it was a few minutes before his wife could continue.

"I used to work as a cook, in a big house near Alexandra Palace, north of the city. The house belonged to a rich man who had no wife, but who loved his money. This man, Mr Edwin Sissington, he paid me very little, as he knew I was foreign and he thought I did not deserve more, but his other servants, his manservant and his housekeeper, he treated much better. He took them with him when he went away, he gave them more money to live on, and they too treated me as a slave. I was very unhappy there, and it was a dream come true when my husband came to take me away."

She looked adoringly up into the eyes of Mr Burgonya.

"Master Edwin may have had no wife, but he did have family. There was a sister, a lovely, cheerful woman, with a husband and—a son. Her name was Joanna. Joanna Dyson."

Eric stared.

"You—you knew my parents?"

Mrs Burgonya smiled gently.

"Yes, I did meet your parents. They did not visit the brother's house often. I think they found Master Edwin too sour, too—unpleasant. He was not a nice man. He must have had much money, but I never saw him spend it, unless it was on himself or his two favourite servants. I never knew why they were so favoured, or so devoted. There must have been something special between them, I think."

Eric was still reeling from the news that she had known his family, even himself as a young child. He took deep breaths and tried to get to grips with the information.

"Right. Let's take this one step at a time. My uncle—Edwin Sissington—what did he do?"

"He was a scientist. He works at a big laboratory in the city, testing out new chemical compounds for governments all over the world. He is a very knowledgeable man, and has to be secretive, so maybe that is why he is so severe. I still see one of the girls who works there, Lilly the cleaner, who told me one day earlier this year he came home from work in a terrible rage, saying his technicians were useless, they should be sacked, for letting one of his most precious experimental rats escape. This rat, it had new DAN or something—"

"Dearest, you mean DNA," corrected her husband quietly.

"Yes, of course, thank you. But that meant it could do things a rat cannot normally do. I hate to imagine what that could be."

Eric did not make the connection. Thickpea did. She, like Eric earlier when he heard about the car crash, experienced a door in her brain flying open, letting a flood of memories, not all of them pleasant, through. The cages, with narrow openings through which they were fed. The men with huge hands lifting her out, jabbing her with a long, pointed needle, so that she felt hot, strange, sick. The hours of running on wheels, down tubes, then being made to sit and watch people, feeling whatever they felt. Then that glorious day, when the cage door was loose, the chance of freedom given and not refused. The long, hard chase along floorboards, through guttering, out into the sewer system, and on until she reached—Eric. No wonder she had been nervous when she saw him for the first time. Yet, the fear hadn't lasted for more than a few seconds. She could read him, she knew he was no threat. Oh yes, she knew. She was that rat.

Eric reached up with his hand to touch the pocket where she lay, trembling. He could tell she was disturbed, but had no idea why, so he just tried to soothe her by stroking his pocket. Mr Burgonya saw him and felt a shiver of sweat dribble down the back of his neck. This must be the same animal that had appeared in his shop.

"So," Mrs Burgonya continued with her tale, "to explain why I tell you all this now, it was when that man came to the shop last time you visited us. You remember, the blond man?"

Eric nodded. He was unlikely to forget.

"Well, I have seen him before. At your uncle's house. He was the son of the manservant, Chamberlain. He used to come round to see his father whenever he needed money, or somewhere to hide out for a few days, but I never found out why. He is trouble, that young man. Stay away from him, Eric. Do not attempt to get involved with anything he may be doing."

Eric nodded. So he had an uncle, and he seemed to be trying to set him up for something—is that what it is? From what Bonnet had passed on of Newton's story, tiny little pieces of jigsaw were beginning to fit together.

By the time Mr and Mrs Burgonya dropped Eric back at the hostel steps, the Christmas lights were blazing from every lamp-post and shopfront. Old Yar and Winnie were entering as he arrived, both labouring under the weight of their belongings that neither could bear to leave behind. Winnie looked preoccupied and rather upset about something, frowning deeply as she waddled along, while Old Yar was oblivious to everything and everyone, as usual. Bonnet brought up the rear, donning a splendid bowler hat that she kept for her rare trips to the city. She walked with a straight back, swinging her arms vigorously as she strode purposefully onward, looking straight ahead and ignoring everybody she passed, despite the odd looks she was getting. Thickpea was beginning to hold Bonnet in very high regard. She had great spirit, her dark, rat-tail hair, pudgy nose and huge, brown eyes miraculously transformed into any number of faces simply by changing headgear. If she were not so devoted to Eric, the rat could see herself being content to live with the maid.

"Good evening, all," Adrian welcomed them as they emerged from the revolving door into the brightly lit hall. "Good to see you. Know where to go?"

Eric nodded, too full of thought and confused emotions to speak, and made his way, closely followed by Old Yar, through a further door, up a flight of stairs. They were shown into a dormitory of beds by another pimply youth, this time a chubby, cheerful individual with a flashing Christmas tree badge pinned to his t-shirt. He found a bed at the far end of the room, close to a large window that would have overlooked the street below, had it not been just as filthy as those downstairs.

The room straight ahead of the front door was large, with rows of benches and tables set out, and the clatter of hundreds of knives, forks and spoons filled the air. As far as Eric could see, row upon row of tatty, unwashed men were seated, each one tucking into what must have been the first hot meal for a long time. Nobody talked, or even looked up, all concentration directed at cleaning the plates and bowls so that not a crumb or smear of food was left. Having dumped their precious few belongings on two empty beds in the dormitory, Eric and Old Yar joined a long queue, and were soon given a tray, which was duly filled, and made their way to a gap in the ranks of vagrants so they could eat their fill. Thickpea stayed in Eric's pocket, waiting for the morsels he passed up from time to time. She also saw him push a piece of crusty bread into another pocket, saving it for a future time—a habit adopted by all street dwellers as an insurance against hunger.

They sat amongst a huddle of filthy men, many of whom seemed very old but actually may not have been more than a few years older than Eric, but all of whom smelled more strongly than any sewer Thickpea had ever encountered. They ate their rations with a determination and speed, and series of slurps and belches that was most unbecoming, and made no attempt to make friends with Eric or the old sailor. By contrast, Eric ate sedately, savouring each mouthful—the meat and gravy, then hot potatoes, even the soggy green vegetables that were impossible to identify. Old Yar attempted to strike up a conversation with his nearest neighbours, explaining how to repair a bilge pump in a force nine gale after a meal of seagull stew—"it tastes just as good on the way back up, don't you know,"—but he received only grunts, and not very many of them, so he gave up and concentrated on his meal. Thickpea wondered if it was the same in the women's dining room, and what would Bonnet be wearing for the occasion? A chef's hat, perhaps, or that old Pizza Parlour baseball cap she had, or maybe a Santa Claus hat to match the time of year? The rat munched contentedly in her hiding place, imagining the range of possibilities.

As they finished eating, Eric and Old Yar took their trays to a cleaning-up table, then made their way to the dormitory. Eric removed his jacket with Thickpea still in the pocket, slipped it over the back of a chair, and put his finger to his lips, indicating that she should stay put and keep quiet. He then picked up a large, fluffy towel that lay at the end of the bed, and went off for a hot shower. It was tempting to go and explore, but the rat was afraid of being seen, so snuggled down and slept until Eric returned, smelling of soft fruit and with a warm glow of comfort in his eyes. He fell asleep almost the instant his head touched the pillow, which surprised Thickpea, as it normally took a while to get used to comfort; it was a sign of how exhausted Eric was after the mess of recent events.

16

Red Hot Pinpricks

Christmas Eve

Next morning, the men joined the women for breakfast in the dining hall, and Eric made his way through the lines of hungry faces to sit beside Bonnet, with Winnie on her other side. They soon fell into conversation, with Bonnet straightening a little felt hat bedecked with cherries that was a little too large and kept slipping over her eyes. Her shoulders were hunched, and Thickpea got the feeling she was trying to blend in with the old bag ladies that surrounded them. When Eric mentioned Blondie, she winced, obviously still very upset after her abduction ordeal; Eric noticed and changed the subject without delay.

"So how was the journey here?" he asked innocently, making polite conversation.

"Oh, it was alright, I suppose," replied Winnie, buttering a piece of toast so thickly that the bread was invisible, "but I would so have preferred a chauffeur, but it would have to be one without a moustache. You never can tell what people are thinking behind a moustache. And the walk did me some good, you know. It's my back. It's quite an effort getting in and out of vehicles these days, what with my plum sago."

They chattered on merrily. Winnie started talking to her other neighbour, a tall man with dark-rimmed sunglasses and a woolly hat pulled right over his ears, and she saw them comparing coats and clothing, as if each were trying to outdo the other in the number of layers they were wearing. Bonnet paused in her gossiping and took a deep breath.

"You know, Eric, I dream about my time in the house."

Eric looked at her. Clearly she was ready to talk about it. He kept silent, leaving her to choose her moment to speak. They munched their toast and marmalade for a few minutes, then Bonnet spoke again.

"He didn't hurt me, but it was the things he said that scared me. He seemed to know all about you, your home, your—family. I'd never asked you about them. That was always a private thing. But now I understand why you're here."

Eric put his toast down and turned slowly to look into her eyes. They were big, brown, bottomless pits of sadness, damp with emotion, and he couldn't stop himself from blinking, to hold back his own tears. She spoke hastily.

"Don't worry, I wouldn't tell a soul. If you want, I'll forget what I heard, but I don't know how. And he kept asking me what I could tell him about you—where you lived when you were not with the rest of us, if you had a routine, where you hang out during the day. He got angry once, when I wouldn't say where we all met, you know, at the Mansions. I did not give us away, you must believe me."

Eric nodded slowly. He trusted this lass and felt calm, even after what she had told him.

"I heard him on the phone once or twice, talking to a man called Bob. He said, "Let Gran sort that out. She's in the right place." It was odd, you know. Something he said rang a faint bell, but—oh, it's probably nothing."

"Go on," encouraged Eric.

"Well," Bonnet leaned back in her chair, screwing up her face to remember it exactly, "he said his grandmother suffered—from asteroids."

Eric sat up straight. He stared into the distance, his mind working overtime. Some important bits of the mystery had just become all too clear. Then, without saying another word, he rose from his chair and walked to the door, Thickpea still secure in his pocket nest but feeling tiny red-hot pinpricks on the soles of her paws as she sensed Eric's rage. There was somebody the boy needed to contact.

As the queues for breakfast dwindled and time moved towards morning coffee time, Old Yar had been absorbed into

the company of men who now had clean, neatly shaven beards
and freshly scented clothes, as they all began to relax a little,
their normal reluctance to talk freeing up and the flood of stories now unstoppable. He told of his own past, he listened to
the gems of the other homeless old men who each had a history
of their own, he laughed out loud at their antics, he made them
guffaw with his tales of rounding the Horn in a teaspoon or living off puffin droppings when all other food had run out. The
yarns became more and more unbelievable as the day wore on,
but the evident joy on the faces of the audience kept the flow of
tall tales pouring freely. There was no sign of Eric.

Winnie and Bonnet took their time cleaning themselves and
their belongings. Bonnet made the most of the opportunity to
wash every one of her precious hats, then brushing each one lovingly to restore it to pristine condition. Winnie, still looking
rather pale and preoccupied, scrubbed her clothes so hard that
her hands were red raw when she had finished. She seemed to be
scrubbing to remove something deeper than dirt. When she was
satisfied, which was not until much later in the day, she carefully folded everything up and placed it with great care back in
the Harrods and Argos bags she had brought with her. Adrian's
girlfriend, Rachel, had offered her new bags to keep her stuff in,
but she refused them curtly.

"I don't know where they've been. I could catch all sorts of
anthracites."

This stumped Rachel, until Bonnet whispered that the old
woman meant parasites, and was always getting her words
wrong. Rachel smiled and accepted this explanation as if it was
quite normal for people to suffer from coal-related problems.

The rest of the day was taken up with a range of domestic
tasks, with each of the world-weary visitors taking their time

rekindling old friendships and sorting out their belongings. A doctor, a dentist and a chiropodist were on hand to sort out any ailments; a pile of donated clothing and essential bits and pieces was rooted through by dozens of pairs of hands, the first in the queue getting some very posh items. One bag lady, known as Tofu Lil, walked out a few days later wearing a coat with a fancy fur collar and a pair of fur-lined leather boots, as well as a woolly hat in bright pink. Adrian, who was in charge of the clothes counter when she attacked it with gusto, was a little worried when he saw her leave the room with so many desirable objects. He suspected she would be mugged within hours of leaving the hostel, and left with nothing. He must have a word with somebody about that.

What these homeless folk, who relied on the hostel for a Christmas respite, did not realise, was the organisation and dedication of the small band of volunteers who manned it. Adrian was just one of ten who did their utmost to make the short stay as pleasant as possible, to prepare each person a little better for their life on the streets, and to make sure they were fit enough to cope by themselves. Every year classes were given on self-defence, how to avoid drugs, how to get off drugs, where to find a trustworthy person to talk to, getting a job, and the law relating to living on the streets. Both men and women were encouraged to help in the preparation of the meals, in an attempt to show them how to cook, and a few of the younger homeless helped in the laundry, where they learned about personal hygiene and the types of wildlife that enjoy living on people. Their time at the hostel was inevitably short, as it closed just after New Year's Day, with every one of the guests being gently eased back onto the streets hopefully better prepared and with a possible future to aim for. Some made it out of the cycle of homelessness; most didn't. They were the ones that came back the following year.

Eric left the building, Thickpea safely in his pocket. He was looking for a telephone, fingering the few coins he had in his pocket as he walked, his mind swirling with all the information whirlpooling around it.

The nearest phone box was on the opposite side of the road, and after nearly ending up under the wheels of a black taxi that dashed along Liverpool Street, presumably taking some last minute shopper to Oxford Street. The driver blasted his horn, but Eric simply waved merrily as he loped over the road. Reaching the phone box, he pulled a business card out of his pocket and read it aloud. Thickpea peeped through the torn seam, listening.

"John Bagnall, Insurance Broker"—followed by an e-mail address and two phone numbers. Eric dialled one of the numbers, the one for a mobile phone.

The ringing did not last long. John Bagnall answered.

"Hello?"

"Is that—Belt?"

"Eric?"

"I need to talk."

"Of course. I had a feeling it wouldn't be long. I've got news for you too. Look, I can't talk here—give me half an hour. You know the bank on the corner, next to the station? It's—Peter's Bank, with the flame as a logo."

"Yes. I know it. Half an hour then."

The phone went dead. Eric meandered away from the phone box, thinking quietly to himself.

Thickpea's skin prickled with a touch of fear. Those instructions about meeting by a bank, near a station—it unsettled the rat. How did Belt know where Eric was?

17

Headlines

Eric wandered slowly up to Liverpool Street Station. With half an hour to wait, he had time to sight-see, looking at the shops and the people milling around the concourse, each one heading somewhere with a purposeful stare and blinkers. Passing each shop in turn, he fondled the ties on the racks, picked up travel brochures, and inspected the croissants with a critical eye as if they weren't fresh enough. He thought he saw a familiar face—yes, he knew one lady who stood close to the escalators, her face so well known from the giant posters he had seen advertising an expensive perfume. She glanced at Eric briefly as he passed, or rather, she glanced through him, as if he were transparent. He smiled sadly. Invisibility was what Eric always aimed for, but this time it would have been nice to have been noticed.

As they passed a newsagent's stand, a headline on a free newspaper caught Thickpea's eye. She squeaked softly, and when Eric looked at her, she stared down at the sign.

"Sissington Laboratories sign Government Contract."

Eric picked up one of the papers and flicked through to find the story as he moved away, heading back to Peter's Bank to keep his appointment with Belt. He read aloud but in a whisper, so that Thickpea heard it too.

"The experimental laboratory based in Liverpool Street, the Sissington Laboratories, has won a government contract to work on a new form of medical treatment that can change the DNA of the patients. Very few details are being released, as the threat of scientific and industrial espionage are considerable, but our reporter has managed to speak briefly to Horace Sprockett, one of the lab technicians."

There was a rather blurred photograph of a greasy, fat man wearing a white coat and holding out his hand as if trying to hide his face from the camera. The story continued.

"The emphasis is on curing long-term illnesses, according to Doctor Edwin Sissington, the chief research scientist at the laboratory, by encouraging the patient's body to heal itself. If successful, it will revolutionise the world of medicine, and many existing drugs may become obsolete."

That was all it said. It had been a huge headline for such a short snippet of story. But what a story! Eric took the sheet with the story on it, unravelled it from the rest of the newspaper, and popped it into his shoulder bag. The rest of the paper went into the nearest waste bin. Eric looked around him, as if checking to see if he could be overheard, and murmured to Thickpea, "And I dare say they needed rats to test their drugs on, am I right?"

A shudder from the pocket told him that he was.

"And that man? The one in the photo?"

Another shudder.

"The—"

Eric used a swear word that caused a passing lady to turn round and say, "Well, really!" in an affronted voice. Eric didn't care. His face was fixed in a grim glare as he faced the modern, glass-fronted office block that housed Sissington Laboratories. Nobody should be allowed to do any harm to any creature. His hand was still cradled gently over Thickpea's pocket, and he didn't immediately notice that he was not alone.

A hand touched his shoulder. Eric spun round and came face to face with the vagrant who had been sitting beside Winnie during breakfast. He still wore the dark-rimmed sunglasses and the woolly hat that came right over his ears; but Eric knew him this time.

"Hello, Eric."

"Belt. Hi. Silly of me not to recognise you this morning."

"I'll take it as a compliment. You weren't supposed to know me."

They walked along slowly, past the station, towards Sissington Laboratories. Eric talked quickly, going through the set-up over the kidnap, some of which Belt knew; then what he had learned about his family, and what he had found out about

Thickpea. The rat even looked out of her pocket and squeaked a hello to Belt, who curtly nodded his response.

"Yes, I know some of that too. I'm sorry I couldn't help with your being accused of the kidnaps—I needed to hide Ellie away, couldn't risk her getting taken again, so we had to disappear for a while. But as for the rest, I need to dig deeper, though—can you leave it with me?"

"But I—"

"I know, you want answers now, yes? Well, in my line of work, I like to get things absolutely right before committing myself. So let me keep on it for another day, okay?"

Eric was silent. This wasn't what he had wanted to hear. Belt sighed.

"Look, your family is mixed up in some unpleasant stuff. It goes deeper than you know. Some of it is a danger to the public, and all of it is for profit and fame. Just let me say, it's your uncle I'm after, and I'm not quite there yet. I need your patience—I can't have you going in messing it all up."

"I'm not going to—"

"No, I know you're not. Okay, here's one thing you can do. Go to St. Thomas' Hospital. It's near Westminster Bridge. The opposite side of the river from Parliament. Find Ward K2."

"What on earth for?"

"You'll see when you get there. You're looking for the coma man."

"The—what?"

"Not a what, a who. The coma man. He's in a side ward, off K2. I'm not saying any more now. You give me time, and it'll all come right. Deal?"

Eric looked into the firm gaze in front of him, and decided.

"Deal," he said, and turned to walk away. When he looked over his shoulder a moment later, Belt had vanished. One day, Eric promised himself, he'd find out what that man really did for a living. Insurance broker? I don't think so, he adjudged.

18

The Coma Man

The walk down to the city was long and cold. The gold-tinged sky threatened snow, but was holding on to it until either there was enough of it to make it worth its while and cause a blizzard, or until Christmas Day arrived, less than a day away. Eric walked briskly, hands in pockets, anonymous as usual but also cleaner and more acceptable to the passing crowds, so he did not need to try to be invisible, he just was. One of the everyday folk of London. It felt comfortable, and he sensed a touch of freedom in not having to try to not be there.

Past Somerset House, the Halls of Justice, the Olde Cheshire Cheese pub—all buildings that rang bells in his memory but Eric did not know why. He came upon Trafalgar Square quite suddenly, Nelson's Column having been well hidden behind the tall office blocks that surrounded the area. The Square itself was busy, as expected, with gaggles of tourists from all corners of the globe taking photos, reading guidebooks, buying souvenirs. The bustle was exhilarating. Eric felt proud of his city.

He headed down Whitehall, past the soldiers in Busbies on their magnificent horses, and was tempted to stop and stare—but Belt's enigmatic coma man was too much of a draw. He had to keep going to find at least some of the answers.

St. Thomas' Hospital lay below the level of the street, down a flight of steps and across a car park. It took Eric a while to find his way around the labyrinth of corridors, but he found the lifts and waited for one to arrive. He got in, along with two men in white coats and a woman with a small boy whose head was swathed in bandage, and they all exited on floor D. As soon as they were alone, Thickpea dashed down Eric's arm and pressed the 'K' button.

Eric smiled.

"Clever little devil, aren't you?"

Thickpea felt a warm glow flood up from her toes. The lift moved almost silently, rushing upwards without any sensation of movement at all. The door opened on floor K, and they walked out into the pastel-painted corridor, with pictures of gardens and stately homes decorating the walls. A doorway on the left was labelled 'K1', then another had 'K2' on the door; a set of double doors swung open onto another corridor from which many small rooms led off. Eric wandered by, looking in each room in turn, his search uninterrupted by nurses or orderlies asking what he was doing there. A nurse's desk loomed ahead of him, and he nipped into a side ward and hid behind a curtain that had been pulled round one of the beds. He waited for a moment to make sure he had not been seen, then turned to see who occupied the bed.

A man lay there. His face was peaceful, as if asleep, his arms and legs quite still, his hair brushed and clean. A bank of machines whirred and hummed behind him, and several wires and tubes stuck out of his arm. Eric approached him slowly, a strange expression on his face. He reached out his hand and touched the man's cheek. Thickpea's extra-sensory abilities went into overdrive. Her feet twitched uncontrollably, and her breath came in short gasps. This was a new sensation for her. She had no idea what on earth it meant.

There was no response from the man to Eric's touch. Looking above the bed head, Eric saw the label, "Tom Dyson. Nil by mouth." Thickpea's shaking became more intense; she was slipping down inside the pocket, unable to hold her place at the top where she had been looking out. But at least it made sense now. This was Belt's coma man. It was Eric's dad.

So this was the man who had been driving the car that had veered off the road and killed his mother. Eric had felt so much anguish and remorse, that he had fled the scene and abandoned his home, preferring an anonymous life on the streets. And his father had been here ever since, in a coma, unable to blame Eric for anything, unable to tell him off, unable to forgive him. Time had frozen the boy's chance to apologise, to put things right. Thickpea, using all her strength to overcome the shaking and pull herself to the top of her pocket, stared into the coma man's face. She saw a kind man, without any malice in his brow, no cruelty or vengeance on his lips, but a deep sadness engrained in every feature. He was at peace, yet in a state of limbo, unable to carry on living as he had lost his family, so waiting, for some small miracle that would end his sleep. Thickpea remembered what Eric had hinted about his childhood, his selfish manner, always demanding more, creating a scene when he didn't get his own way, yelling and hitting out whenever thwarted. It must have been so difficult for this man, who had made a home that should be happy and had so many comforts, but who had to endure a constant barrage of self-centred greed from the son he loved. A dull ache in Thickpea's chest weighed her down. It was worse than any sorrow she had ever felt, and she was sure she was feeling the combined torment of both father and son.

Eric sat down heavily in a chair beside the bed. A tear trickled down his cheek. Thickpea moved down onto his lap, nestling in his hands to give him what little comfort she could.

"Dad, oh dad, if only I could—"

Eric sighed, and with the tears streaming down his face now, he began to talk.

"I only ran because it was my fault. I still—loved you—but it was the guilt. I knew it was my shouting that made you look back, made you hit that tree, get mum—killed. I couldn't face you after that, or Uncle Edwin, having got his sister killed. That's why I hid myself away. I didn't want to be found, I never wanted to see any of you again. My life vanished that day, and what I am now is somebody else. I don't shout now, Dad, you must believe me, I don't rave and pout like I used to. I saw what it did to my family. I'll not do that again."

He tipped Thickpea into his lap, reached forward and took his father's hand in his own.

"You do understand, don't you? I can tell you loads of stuff about my new life, it's been not that bad overall. But I need your help now, Dad. There's something going on, and I don't understand it. Look, do you mind if I talk it through? I'm not sure you can hear, but all the same—"

And Eric went on to tell him all about what had been happening over the past weeks—Bonnet's disappearance, how Blondie kept turning up, Belt and his part in it all, the way Eric was being set up, the days at the hostel, Mrs Burgonya—and, the most baffling bit, how his uncle kept cropping up in the mystery.

"So there it is, dad. All a bit confusing, and me in the middle. Any ideas?"

Then a tiny miracle happened. Eric gave a gasp, and he glanced down to where his hand held that of his father. The fingers of the man's hand had tightened around those of his son, as he squeezed. The smallest acknowledgement, but an important one for both of them. Thickpea's shaking stopped immediately, replaced by a soaring, glorious warm happiness, topped off with a dizzying lightness in her head that made her think she was flying. In an almost invisible instant, the father had returned to the son, and the family was together again after so many years of loneliness and sorrow.

19

Rogue in the Family

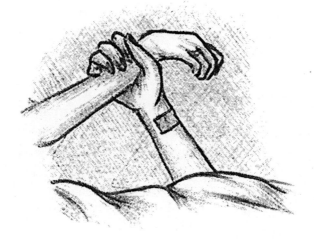

The moment of euphoric peace was broken abruptly as the curtains were swished back and a nurse appeared, wearing a stiff blue uniform and an even stiffer expression, her sharp nose and pointed chin adding to the dour image. She looked down at Eric with disdain. She did not spot the rat snuggling in the folds of Eric's lap. Thickpea endeavoured to keep it that way and did not budge.

"Ah, yes, I thought it was you," she said quietly, her voice with a hard edge that matched the pointed features of her face. "I've been listening to you wittering on for ages. What a load of balderdash you've been saying, boy. He can't hear a thing anyway, you know. Quite unconscious to everything, been like it for—oh, four years now. But you know that, don't you?"

Eric froze. He held onto his father's hand, anger coursing through him. He noticed her nametag—Staff Nurse Audrey Butler. Miss A. Butler.

"What do you want with my dad?"

"What a stupid question," she sneered at him. "I'm here to look after these people, including your father." She said these last two words with a loud emphasis and a snarl. "I should be asking you the same question."

"I wanted to talk—and he squeezed my hand—"

"Nonsense, boy," the nurse busied herself straightening pillows and tidying the bed sheets. "This man's not made any sign of movement for years. You were dreaming. People often imaging things like this when they long for something to happen. He's not in any pain, you know. He'll probably remain like this for the rest of his life."

"How do you know?" Eric cried, feeling suddenly defensive about his father, "How do you know what he feels? How can you tell how much pain he's in, if he can't tell you? And what about mental pain, the misery of knowing his wife is gone, his son is lost—how do you know he can't feel that?"

"Dear me, we are getting carried away," Nurse Butler's smile was ugly. "A few minutes at his bedside, and you're an expert, eh?"

She leaned over to check Tom Dyson's breathing and pulse. Eric did not move. Thickpea took the opportunity to scramble up into his pocket, out of view, moving so fast that any onlooker would have seen no more than a brown blur.

"I know you," he said softly.

Staff Nurse Butler laughed. He continued.

"It was a long time ago. I remember—a big house, my uncle Edwin, having afternoon tea, mum and dad were there, and you—you served the cakes. You were my uncle's housekeeper."

"Mmm, what a good memory, boy," murmured the nurse, looking at her watch pinned to her uniform as she took her patient's pulse.

"Mrs. Butler. Yes, I remember you. You were always going on about your nursing training, saying it made you an ideal person to look after such a good, public-spirited man as my uncle. Mum used to laugh about you whenever we got back home, though she didn't know I saw her doing it. She said you should have been Uncle Edwin's sister instead of her. They never really got on, did they?"

"Got on? Of course they never got on, you stupid boy. Your mother, that great man's baby sister. Who was so pretty as a child, so talented, always good at ballet, singing, making people laugh. She was the apple of every eye in the room whenever she appeared. Your uncle? He was the brainy one, always had his head stuck in a book, no time for the niceties of life. He wanted to achieve something, wanted to make his name in the world doing something great, something that could change lives. And he has so nearly made it, after years of toil in that laboratory of his. He's so close, it's only a matter of time—until that damn rat escaped."

Eric hid his shock at this statement.

"How can his whole plan be ruined be one measly rat?" he mocked, silently apologizing to Thickpea for the insult. He felt her wriggle—she knew he didn't mean it.

"The rat that got away was the one with the right formula, of course." Nurse Butler finished taking Tom Dyson's pulse and smoothed her uniform as she spoke. "The years of experimentation to get it right, and when he manages it—"

"Manages what, exactly?"

The nurse looked nervous for the first time.

"That's confidential."

"Come on, I'm family, remember? What threat can I be now?" Eric opened his eyes wide, trying to look more innocent than he felt.

She glared at him, then shrugged.

"You'll not be telling anybody anything, I can guarantee that."

Thickpea's shaking started again.

"It is a chemical that enables a person, or creature, to read—well, not thoughts, exactly, but emotions. That rat had shown she could sense anger, fear, pain, joy. It read the reactions of the people nearby. It responded differently to each feeling—shaking when it felt fear, scratching its nose meant confusion, a rise in body temperature when somebody was happy. There were others, I don't remember them all. My master called it an empathy scanner."

Eric didn't reply. He thought about Thickpea's skills of reading his own feelings, and knew that without realising it, he knew more about this experiment's results than Nurse Butler, the assistant of his beloved uncle, did. He knew what his rat was capable of. As he stood, staring at the comatose figure of his father lying on the bed, attached to a battery of machines by wires and tubes that ticked and pinged at regular intervals, he suddenly felt afraid, for Thickpea, for his father and for himself. By telling him as much as she had, Nurse Butler had condemned them all. He kept her talking, trying to delay any threat being carried out, and also to make the most of her talkative mood to find out more.

"But—why try to get at me? Why is my uncle so against me? What have I ever done to him?"

Nurse Butler reached into her pocket.

"You are your mother's son. He grew to detest her, and anybody connected with her. You are guilty, simply by being there."

"And what do you get out of it all?"

"Ah, well, I'll say this for your Uncle Edwin—he rewards loyalty with uncommon generosity. My brother Robert and I—"

"Brother? You have an accomplice?"

Nurse Butler burst into hysterical laughter. She leaned on the edge of the bed and shook with mirth. It took a few minutes for her to calm down.

"Oh, you do me too much honour, boy. I couldn't do all this. No, my family has close links with the Sissington household. My brother is Master Edwin's manservant, I am his housekeeper, my mother was his nanny, my nephew is the handyman. This medical breakthrough, financed by the government who think it'll cure millions of long-term sick world-wide, know nothing of this, er, interesting and potentially lucrative side effect. It may well do just that, curing previously fatal conditions, but that's not the moneymaking side. We will all become immensely rich if my master manages to persuade some less honest and caring country to buy and use the empathy scanner in their dealings with terrorists, or rebel groups, or deadly enemies. And your uncle will not let us go unrewarded. See what I am trying to say?"

The penny was beginning to drop. The Butler family was in on the scam, to get the government to pay for research that will net them a healthy profit while providing some foreign power with a weapon to read the weaknesses of their enemies, and that may, as a by-product, cure some nasty life-threatening illnesses. Uncle Edwin was the chief research scientist and mastermind behind the plot, and as far as Eric could see, he would benefit both in terms of fame, the saviour of so many ailing people, and in terms of wealth, from the illegal sales of the chemical abroad. But—

"I still don't see how I come into it," Eric frowned, sitting back in the chair as he tried to figure it all out.

"Ah, well, there is something else you don't know, boy. Your uncle, great man as he is, must succeed in finding a life-saving drug, for his own survival. He has been diagnosed with a cancer, and has only months to live."

He had a feeling he ought to be upset at this news, but all he could feel was the beginnings of a light at the end of a long, dark tunnel.

"And," Eric's mind began to kick into gear, "if he dies, then—"

"You will be his heir, yes," growled Nurse Butler, her eyes screwed into tight slits of venom as she watched Eric. "You will inherit everything he has worked so hard to get. You are his sole surviving relative, and due to a family covenant, he cannot change the conditions of his will. If you were out of the picture, then he would be free to pass his worldly goods to anybody he wished—us, for instance."

"But I haven't been attacked, not physically anyway," Eric's confusion returned. "Just the attempt to set me up for the kidnapping, that's all."

"Think about it, boy. That was the condition of the will. Not your death, just your disgrace. No person who had any criminal record can inherit in the Sissington family. It's all because of some rogue in the family in the nineteenth century, who swindled a load of money from a family member, then fled the country, leaving the Sissingtons destitute for several generations. It is through the family determination and fortitude that their situation improved, but not as far as Master Edwin had liked. So began his lifelong mission to make a name for himself, and a fortune in the process. So you see, boy, your family were in his way. It would have been solved four years ago, if my brother had done his job right."

Eric sat bold upright.

"Meaning?"

Nurse Butler grinned maliciously.

"You don't think the brakes on your father's car failed just by themselves, do you? You really are more stupid than I expected."

"But—" Eric spluttered, "I thought—it was me—"

"Oh, don't make yourself more important than you really are, boy. Your bad behaviour was a great excuse, though. All we had to do was mention to the police and coroner that you were always arguing with your parents and maybe that had caused the crash. They never bothered to look too closely at the brakes. You and your temper did us a favour."

Eric's body was rigid with horror, the only movement being Thickpea's continued shaking in his pocket. He had spent four years believing he was the reason his mother was dead, he had run away from his comfortable existence to live on the streets of London, all for a lie. This woman, standing in front of him, was proudly announcing that he helped them in the plot to kill them all.

"But we didn't all die. I ran, and dad—"

"Yes, that was a bit of a problem. It's taken all this time for Master Edwin to find the correct formula, and we had found you, been keeping a watch on you for a while now—"

"What do you mean?"

"You'll find out soon enough. Right now, though, I have other things to finish. So if you don't mind—"

With a jerk, Nurse Butler pulled one of the tubes out of Tom Dyson's arm, then turned to one of the machines, the one that regulated the ventilator, and turned the dial to 'off'. Then she systematically removed every other wire from his arm and chest, and pulled out the other ends from each monitor in turn. There was no way to put them all back in the right places without considerable time and knowledge.

An alarm sounded, a shrill squeal that warned of a malfunction in the equipment, waking Eric from the amazed stupor at everything he had heard. He leapt up, grabbed the nurse's arm and pulled her away, uttering a scream of despair as he saw what she had done.

"No! Get away, leave him, don't you touch him ..."

He managed to heave her away from the bedside, and throwing her to the floor with a strength he didn't know he had, he stepped over her to reach the wires, grabbing a handful and staring at them helplessly.

"No, there must be a way. How about this ... no, or this ... no ... how could she, Dad, can you hear me? Dad!"

Tom Dyson lay perfectly still, not responding to the desperate cries of his son, his eyes tight shut and features quite still. A single high-pitched note still howled through the room, and the red lines of peaks and troughs flattened out, so that all that was left was a straight red line. Tom was dying.

"No!" screamed Eric, grabbing his father's hand and rubbing it, trying to coax life back into him. From behind him on the floor came a cruel laugh, hollow and deep.

"Too late, my boy," she crooned, slowly rising up and straightening her uniform. "By the time the crash team get here, it'll be over."

"What? What's a crash team?"

As if responding to the signal, a team of doctors and nurses shot through the door, dragging a huge trolley with even more machines and equipment on it. The sudden entrance of more people caught Thickpea's attention, and, forgetting to keep out of view, she stuck her head out from where she had been hiding in Eric's pocket. The staff nurse looked, and gave a self-satisfied, smug sigh. She knew who Thickpea was. She had all the answers to her problems here in this room.

Nurse Butler reacted like a mad woman. She launched herself at Eric, her hands outstretched, aiming for his neck, screaming, "It's him! He went wild! He must be stopped!" The nurses were trying to help the coma man, and this sudden distraction drew their attention. Nurse Butler had landed on the boy, knocking him backwards into the trolley, her hands still squirming for his throat. Eric struggled, trying to loosen the woman's grasp that was getting tighter, stopping his breathing, turning his face blue, slowly squeezing the life from his body.

It was time for another minor miracle. A hand shot up from nowhere, grabbed one of Nurse Butler's arms, and held it firmly. The grip around Eric's neck was broken, and he crumpled to the floor. The staff nurse was standing stock still, staring at the hand, then at the man lying on the bed, who had reached out to protect his son.

"But—you can't—it's not possible—" she stammered, as the hand fell back to the bed and Tom Dyson looked comatose once again. His eyes had never opened, he had made no sound. But he had just saved Eric.

Eric was swept into the arms of one of the nurses, with a reassuring "Come along now, son, we'll sort him out," and he was ushered out into the corridor before he realised what had happened. A scream issued from Nurse Butler as she tried to explain her actions to the crash team at the top of her voice, obviously having some difficulty getting them to believe her story.

"But I told you! It was him! Him and that rat! Didn't you see it? Sitting in his lap, comfy as you like, just watching—it was there? What do you mean, am I on medication? I am not hallucinating, stupid girl. I'm a nurse, no, not on this ward, but does that matter? It was that boy, don't you see? No, of course I don't know why he'd kill his own father—"

Eric didn't listen any more. He sat on the floor with his hands over his ears, shutting out her yells and shrieks, his mind fuzzy with despair at the thought of finding then losing his father in a matter of minutes. He didn't think he could take much more. A few minutes later, Staff Nurse Butler was led out of the side ward, still howling her innocence and her accusations against Eric and Thickpea—whom the doctors were convinced did not exist—as they took her away.

20

Bare Windows

Minutes turned into hours. The seats in the corridor of Ward
K2 were not designed to be sat in for hours, and Eric was getting numb; but he didn't care. It matched the dull emptiness in

his head, which got deeper and more impenetrable the more he thought of what had happened that day. He wondered if anybody at the hostel was worried about him, if Bonnet had organised a search party yet, or whether she was too busy with the festive preparations. Pictures flitted in and out of his mind; a doctor passing down the corridor at a run, holding a pager and reaching for his stethoscope; a couple of visitors wandering through, saying, "He said he was in K2 ward, but I can't see anybody here with a saucepan stuck on their head," then plodding towards the nurses' station to ask for directions; the nurse coming out of his father's room, sitting next to him, putting an arm around him and saying, "I'm sorry, but your father passed away a few minutes ago. It was very peaceful," then leaving him alone again; Belt turning up and taking the seat next to his without a word. His presence was just enough to let him know that although he may feel lonely, he was not alone.

Thickpea's shaking had stopped. She was exhausted, her tiny body limp and still in the pocket, her breathing coming as tiny gasps. She suddenly felt very tired, her legs ached, her tail lifeless, her whiskers no longer capable of feeling any sensation at all. She lay there in what a human would call a dead faint, completely unaware of what was happening around her.

After a while, an auxiliary brought them sandwiches and a plastic mug of hot chocolate, which they both ate gratefully. Neither of them spoke. Belt knew Eric would say something when he needed to, and knew to keep quiet until he was ready. He was now dressed in normal clothes, not in the wig and glasses that had hidden his true identity from those at the hostel. He was clean shaven, his tall figure slim and athletic, those shrewd grey eyes misted over with tears of sympathy for the young man suffering beside him. Eric was glad he was there.

And now he was dressed like himself, John Bagnall, the boy no longer thought of him as Belt.

The time came for Eric to rejoin the human race, some time after the sandwich break. He sat upright, stretched, and looked sideways towards John Bagnall. With a limp smile, he simple said, "Thanks," then stood and walked to the toilet. When he returned, a few minutes later, his face was washed and his hair pushed back from his face in an attempt to tidy himself up. John stood, and looked him up and down.

"I've news, if you're ready," he said quietly.

Eric looked at him, and nodded.

"Let's finish it."

The laboratory was on the second floor of Sissington Towers, a tower block of stainless steel and glass not far from the station. The remainder of the floors were occupied by other companies that rented them from the Sissington Scientific Group, the research body owned and run by Uncle Edwin. Their company's wealth had grown slowly over the past four years, as the laboratory had been awarded government contracts as well as undertaking research for other financial institutions, testing the safety of cosmetics, household cleaners and car products. As their experience had widened, so had their fame and value flourished, not all of it from positive aspects of their work. The bulk of the testing on new materials involved using animals, and this became a source of great anger within certain animal rights groups. There were regular protests outside the building, as there had been on the day Newton had been slashed with a knife by Sprockett. They were not usually violent, but always noisy, with plenty of chanting "Don't test on animals, they can't answer back" and other slogans. Placards were waved, with pictures of rabbits in tiny cages, or dogs with their eyes red and sore. They made no difference to what went on inside the building. Edwin Sissington had made sure the second floor was soundproof, so no noise could get in—or out.

Eric looked up at the building. Every floor except the second and the penthouse displayed Christmas decorations on or through the windows—snowflakes, tinsel, dangling baubles and fairy lights in the shape of reindeer pulling sleighs. The second floor and the penthouse windows were bare. That was where Edwin Sissington was in charge—the second floor housing his laboratory, and the penthouse apartment being his own home.

There was a small contingent of protesters that day. A short girl with long flowing hair and a brightly coloured headband was trying to stimulate the rest of them into another chant, but the response was rather half-hearted. At the back of the group was Newton, his face still dreadfully marked from his attack, but he seemed to be keeping himself out of the way, until he spotted Eric and John Bagnall approaching. Then he pushed his way through.

"John! There you are!" he grunted. Eric looked from one man to the other. Another small revelation. These two knew each other—they may even be working together.

"Hello, Newton," John replied, patting the deformed shoulder warmly. "Anything new?"

"No," Newton looked round, making sure nobody else was close enough to hear him. "That lout Sprockett is in there, and I've seen Sissington's manservant Chamberlain, so I reckon they're having a council of war. I hear the housekeeper's out of the picture now?"

"Mmm." John looked at Eric. "Your staff nurse has been put in safe keeping, with a police guard. She is accused of murdering your dad, Eric. The way she dismantled his life support system could only have been done by somebody who knew what they were doing. I spoke to the inspector dealing with the matter, and she seems to be singing like a canary, as the phrase goes. Your uncle is going to be in deep trouble any minute now, I reckon, and I'd like to be the first to speak to him."

John nodded his thanks to Newton and his companions, and Eric followed him to the entrance of Sissington Towers. The tiny inert body of Thickpea lay inside his pocket, seemingly unaware of what was happening.

As they reached the door, Eric pulled John back.

"Before we do this," he said urgently, "tell me—why did you call yourself Belt?"

John looked surprised.

"What? You need to know that now?"

Eric smiled, rather self-consciously.

"Well, I'm not sure I'll get much chance to ask you later."

"Good point." John turned to face him. "It's nothing much, I'm afraid. When I first met Old Yar, he pointed out that my trousers were held up with chandler's rope, the sort found on yachts and fishing vessels. He liked the idea of me wearing what he called a seaman's belt—and the name stuck."

"Mmm, that figures," murmured Eric, who grinned briefly before turning back to the entrance of Sissington Towers.

A large glass revolving door led into a huge atrium, clad in marble and chrome, and at a desk at the far end sat a neat, well-groomed lady.

"Can I help you?" she asked politely, looking at John.

"No thank you, we know our way up," he replied, and without waiting for a reply they walked smartly to the lift, pressed the button for the second floor, and got in as soon as the door opened. The receptionist looked a little startled and reached for a phone.

As they exited the lift, John and Eric were confronted by a steel doorway, clearly designed to keep out unwanted guests. By the handle was a key pad, and John punched in a set of numbers. The door opened silently. Eric looked enquiringly up at him.

"I've been here before," John murmured, "only don't tell anybody else that."

They walked through, and into a small reception area. The walls were white and there were no pictures to break up the stark, gleaming cleanliness. This was no hospital corridor, with its pleasant artwork to calm the nerves and distract the fears of those who passed by. Three doors led off the reception, and John went straight to the middle one. He knocked confidently and walked straight in. Eric followed closely behind.

The room was large with a desk beneath the window and several chairs against the walls. A few cabinets decorated the rest of the space, along with a large fish tank and some leafy plants. It looked clinically tidy. Behind the desk sat a large man. He had grey hair, a dark suit and grey tie, and large, metal-framed glasses that made his tiny eyes even smaller were perched on a podgy, pockmarked nose. He worked at a computer, typing and checking figures on a pile of papers at the side of the keyboard. As they entered, he looked up. A change of facial expression, from absorbed-in-work mode to how-did-you-two-get-in-here mode, was unconvincing. He stood up suddenly, pushing his chair backwards in his haste.

"What—"

"Good morning, Doctor Sissington," John Bagnall walked forward confidently, holding his hand out. "Your receptionist downstairs will have warned you of our arrival. I believe we've met before. John Bagnall at your service, on attachment from MI5 to Special Branch, working on the illegal use of chemical substances and the sale thereof to undesirable elements. I believe you have met this young man before?"

21

Cold Obsession

Eric walked forward to greet his uncle.

"Hello, Uncle Edwin," his voice was surprisingly calm and strong. "Long time no see." As he spoke, his pocket twitched visibly. Thickpea had come round, and was quite aware of the grave danger she was now in.

Edwin Sissington stared open-mouthed at his nephew, ignoring the outstretched hand offered by John. His gaze flicked across Eric's face, as if trying to put pieces of a jigsaw together in his mind. Abruptly, he switched on a wide smile that would charm birds from clouds.

"Can it be? Yes, good heavens! My dear boy, where have you been? I've been so worried. And you, John, did you find him for me? My dear fellow, I'm so grateful. Come, you must sit and tell me all. Come on, come on, don't stand on ceremony, my boy. You are family."

Sissington pressed a buzzer on his desk and immediately a door opened and the neat secretary from outside the door came in.

"Yes, sir?"

"Libby, fetch some tea. No—good heavens, this is worth more than tea—send out for some champagne, will you? This man has brought me my nephew back from the dead."

The lady bobbed her head and left. John walked over to the window and stared down at the street below, with its crowd of protesters and at the passing traffic. As he watched, a bus pulled up, and out clambered a host of people, loaded down with megaphones, placards and flags. A procession was also approaching from the direction of the hostel, and John recognised a few significant faces—there was Adrian along with quite a few of the homeless visitors. Old Yar was amongst them, and a slight figure wearing a headband adorned with antlers. Bonnet had dressed for the occasion.

Eric was rooted to the spot. His uncle was behaving as though he had done nothing wrong, as though he knew nothing of the kidnap, the framing, the car crash four years previously that had killed his own sister. Maybe—a doubt crossed Eric's mind. Maybe he didn't know anything about it after all. Maybe it was all the brainchild of that Butler woman and her greedy family, and Uncle Edwin had nothing to do with it. Maybe it was all a misunderstanding, a huge mountain that began life as a molehill and had grown to immense proportions in his brain. Eric sneered. Yeh, sure. Maybe cats laid eggs.

"Sit yourselves down, please," Sissington insisted, ushering Eric and John to two chairs backed against the wall. They glanced at each other, then made themselves as comfortable as they could on the straight-backed seats. Eric was not sure what was going to happen. John, however, looked confident and in control.

"You will have heard about your brother-in-law, Dr. Sissington?" John asked casually.

"My—brother-in-law? You mean this young man's father? The last I heard, he was still in a coma, at St. Thomas' Hospital. Why? What's happened to him?" Sissington leaned back in his chair.

Eric found his voice, cracked and hoarse with seething anger, provoked into speech by the over-placid, cold tone of his uncle's voice.

"He's dead. He died this morning. He was killed, by your housekeeper. Your Mrs. Butler was caught in the act, is now in custody. She'll not be coming back to look after you again for a long, long time."

Sissington's face went through a series of expressions, starting with a sudden spark of glee in his eyes, then changing to an exaggerated appearance of shock, followed closely by a dropped jaw as he let his features fall with an air of sadness and confusion.

"Mrs. Butler? Audrey? What on earth has she done?"

John leaned forward.

"I'm sure she was only following orders, doctor. She went to the hospital with the express wish of ending the life of Tom Dyson. Her first aim was to remove him from the line of inheritance that will take over the millions you hope to earn from your work here in the laboratory, knowing that without any family to pass your wealth to, you would give it to those who served you the most faithfully over the years. And, of course, you were never too fond of the Dyson branch of the family, were you? So Mrs. Butler would consider she was doing you a favour by getting him out of the way. Given the chance, I'm sure she intended a similar fate for Eric too—or, Rick, as you know him."

Rick. So that was his name. It came back to his clogged brain like a single ray of light piercing a dense fog. He had been found by Doldrum, all that time ago, wandering the streets, and she had offered to take him to a safe place. She had asked his name—and when he said 'Rick', she misheard, and he was introduced to the others as Eric. Yet again, for the umpteenth time, Eric wondered what had happened to that kind lady who had helped him when he first took to the streets. Only now his wondering was deeply troubled. Too much had gone terribly wrong around him—had Doldrum been a part of his punishment?

Sissington was still looking bewildered, but Eric watched his eyes. They remained strangely distant and blank, unable to hide the cold obsession that gripped his soul.

"But—that can't be right. You can't believe I would ever give orders of that kind. My work in the lab is to save life, not destroy it, and that has taken precedence over all aspects of my existence for the past months. I have no consideration for old news. I work for a better, healthier future for all of mankind. Anyway, forgive my bluntness, but dear old Tom Dyson was as good as dead. Why should I wish to harm somebody who was no threat to me?"

There was a trace of truth in this, and John faltered. Before he could react, a knock on the door heralded the return of Libby and the champagne, plus three glasses. She left them on Doctor Sissington's desk, and left without a word; but a glance at John told him all he needed to know. Help was on the way.

"He was not going to inherit your fortune when you die?"

Sissington laughed dryly.

"Oh, good grief, what fortune? I have no fortune."

"But you will, when your drug to read emotions is finally ready for production."

The doctor started violently.

"What do you know of that?"

"You may be interested to know that one of your number has a conscience, doctor. Plus the fact that you have been under surveillance for some time. Tell me, doctor, when you were younger, did you ever read any Sherlock Holmes stories?"

Doctor Sissington laughed.

"What are you gabbling on about now, man?"

"Sherlock Holmes needed to recruit hired help from time to time, and he often used the young urchins who ran wild on the streets of London. They could get into corners of the city unnoticed, being considered as non-people. Well, I have used a similar method myself—recruiting vagrants to listen and learn for me. You'd be surprised where a homeless person can wangle an entry—even to the fanciest clubs and houses in the land, begging for scraps, searching for clothing, asking the most innocent questions and getting to some truths that would remain unspo-

ken to any 'real' person. Well, one such vagrant has made a connection with a member of your staff, who has been a valuable
source of information to us. Oh, and one more thing, doctor—the government do not allow any companies the generous
grants and financial support such as you have been granted
without keeping a very careful eye on their investment."

"Hence your involvement?"

John smiled.

"Correct. As you no doubt know, my young daughter Ellie
was kidnapped a few days ago, in an attempt to persuade us to
leave your lab and its unsavoury work well alone. Eric helped
me find and rescue her, as you will also have heard by now. It
was your manservant's family, yet again, who were responsible,
along with Sprockett the henchman—tell me, what does he do
around the lab? I can't see him as the delicate, test-tube and
pipette type of lab technician, to be honest."

Sissington looked annoyed. He was not used to allowing
somebody else to control a conversation.

"He deals with the animals, mostly, and takes care of any
heavy lifting and manual jobs around the building."

"Mmm, that figures. But let me get back to the point. The
government and I would be very interested in knowing the
details of what this emotion-reading drug is capable of."

Sissington's agitation was growing.

"I have no intention of divulging trade secrets to you, sir.
And as for your insinuations of my involvement in any illegal
activities, you had better have proof for them, or you will find
yourself on the wrong end of a lawsuit."

John just laughed out loud.

"Can you hear what is going on outside, Doctor?"

He walked to the window and flung it wide open. The others followed, staring down, open-mouthed. In the distance, the strains of a Salvation Army band playing Christmas carols filtered up to them. Directly below them, a considerable crowd had gathered, bellowing a lusty chant of "Sissington out! Animals in!" that echoed between the tall building lining Liverpool Street. The crowd was waving a host of banners and placards, and although a small contingent of police had arrived to keep them in order, several people ran to the entrance of Sissington Towers and pushed their way through the revolving doors. John turned to wink at Eric. He knew what was about to happen and spoke to the doctor with a calm assurance.

"Your dream of immortality and riches is shattered, Dr. Sissington. Before we arrived here, I contacted my head office and have instructed them to advise the government to cease funding immediately. Special Branch will be taking possession of this laboratory in the very near future. Our computer experts will download your files, our scientists will be examining your experimental results and quarantining all the substances you have produced. The animals that have suffered for your cause will be taken into care, and treated accordingly to improve their quality of life as much as possible. Your communications will be impounded, to check to which foreign powers you have been offering your new emotion-reading drug. Your staff will be questioned, and only after all that has been completed, will you be prosecuted for your treasonable actions. Your secrets will not be worth a thing, Doctor Sissington. It would make it much more pleasant for yourself if you would be good enough to tell us some of the details now."

A flare of anger shot across the doctor's eyes, but his defiance was short-lived. Gripping the arms of his chair, and with an exasperated sigh, he flopped back in his seat.

"I only needed one more day, and you would have been too late. The draught is ready for the final experiment—" He reached for a small blue bottle sitting on his desk, rolling it gently in his hand as he spoke ... "—then I was open to the highest bid from—well, one of several countries, actually. Just imagine, some governments were prepared to pay almost anything to be able to recognise an enemy's weaknesses. All it would take would be a simple scan of the people in a room to show what would really demoralise and destroy them utterly. Such a position of strength, growing out of something so basic and so indefensible ... My potential customers loved the idea, you know. I had offers of millions of dollars, millions! All from a lucky accident, a concoction of chemicals that did something unexpected. This could have provided a very comfortable old age for me and my followers."

"Followers? Do you consider yourself to be the head of a religious sect, or something?" John sounded shocked.

"Why not? My friends have been loyal to my beliefs, and have given their whole livelihoods to helping me achieve my goals. We planned to leave this country, to go somewhere where goody-goody science can't touch us, leaving those power-hungry nations to fight it out between themselves."

Thickpea made a decision. She had a plan to execute. Her role in this matter was not over; but there was something wrong. She felt tired, her legs were aching, her lovely, lush fur was rubbing away every time she brushed against a surface. She had a feeling that she was not going to be around for much longer; but the brave little rat was determined to help her beloved Eric while she still could.

Thickpea sneaked out of Eric's pocket, her safe haven, and silently hurried to the floor down the boy's back, out of view. She crept along the skirting board, hiding by chair legs and the huge filing cabinets that she was sure contained all of Uncle Edwin's secrets, and sneaked out of the room through a tiny gap in the doorway, left slightly open by Libby.

"So what exactly is your breakthrough?" John was determined to persuade the doctor to explain the process. Still sagging in his chair, Eric's uncle spoke in a dull, lifeless tone, his spirit gone.

"The possible cure for some of the world's incurable illnesses would have been any scientist's dream discovery. After many years of working in the field, taking samples from around the world and combining new and unusual ingredients, plus some completely new ones from the rainforests of South America, we found a blend that had all the qualities we looked for. Using the animal testing, we cured malaria, sleeping sickness, typhoid and diphtheria in sixty-eight per cent of cases, plus some of the nastiest, life-threatening cancers, with the remaining showing a marked drop in severity, making it easier to live with and to treat. That particular cure is of special significance to me, although it's not common knowledge."

Eric noticed for the first time the hollows under his uncle's eyes. Here was a man clearly living with a great deal of pain. He felt the faint sense of sympathy filtering through his growing anger, but he suppressed it. This man did not deserve his pity.

"The results were remarkable. Then we started to notice other effects. Some of the test subjects began to react to light in extreme ways, and others could not bear high-pitched sounds. One started to suffer from epileptic fits, then developed a liking—quite incredible, this—for curry-flavoured chocolate. We experimented further, and in many case our animals died horrible, but totally necessary, deaths. Then we had a breakthrough. One rat was given a new combination of doses, and it started to read emotions."

Eric reached up to his pocket. It was empty. He patted it gently—but Thickpea was no longer there.

Dr. Sissington continued to speak, sipping at his champagne as if he did not have a care in the world.

"That rat could read people's feelings, as clearly as if it were the open page of a newspaper. We were just on the verge of refining the drug, and extending the test to include other subjects, when the rat escaped. It was far too much like coincidence. Either the rat had developed a conscience and did not want any part of this, or maybe let out by one of those protesters downstairs who pretend to be animal-friendly but still go home to a meal of hamburgers and chips cooked in beef dripping—or the rat had been stolen.

"The upshot was, we interviewed all the staff, and others working in this building, and we tested the security system, which is one of the best in the country, and found out that no person could have helped that rat get away. The remaining possibility, no matter how improbable, must be true—the rat had chosen to flee. It was more of a breakthrough than we had known, and we hadn't recognised it as such until it was too late. Our one successful experiment had—left the building, shall we say. We had lost the chance to do more tests, and to dissect the rat in question, to examine whatever physical changes had taken place."

Eric flinched at the thought of this man cutting up his beloved Thickpea—a feeling intensified by the worry he felt, not knowing where she was.

There were two other doors in the hallway, one on each side of Thickpea. She lifted her head and sniffed. Through the right-hand one wafted the unpleasant odour of chemicals and disinfectant. Not a room she would enter by choice. The other, however, was scented lightly with the delightful pongs of animals; that was where she needed to be. She scampered over, stuck her head through and took a careful look. The walls were lined with cages, each one containing an assortment of rats, rabbits, dogs and tiny monkeys. At the far end, perched on a stool and reading a newspaper, sat Horace Sprockett, gulping noisily as he drank from a mug. Above his head was a metal box, which bore a large red button. This broke the electrical current that controlled the cage locks, but Thickpea did not know that. She just knew she needed to push that button—but how? Her tired little body felt a wave of exhaustion as she realised she may not be able to complete her task.

Once in the animal room, Thickpea was watching Sprockett. He had no idea she was there, but the rest of the inhabitants of that room knew. They had grown strangely quiet, and every pair of animal eyes was trained on the young rat peering round the door.

Thickpea felt oddly nervous. So much depended on her actions now, and she was still feeling weak. Her energy had been sapped these last few days, and much as she would have liked a bit of a lie-down and a kip, she knew that nobody else could do what needed to be done. She took a long, deep, calming breath, then moved forward slowly, following the line of cages, keeping as much as possible out of Sprockett's line of sight.

Thickpea had not been the only intelligent animal in the lab. Another rat, much larger and darker than she was, recognised that she needed help. He was crouching in a cage close to Sprockett's shoulder, and this rat had been trying to ignore the revolting slurping noises the human made whenever he supped his tea. This strange rat had arrived, free of any bars or locks, and was about to do the impossible—set him and his unfortunate cellmates free. Without warning, the dark rat started to squeal hysterically, running round his cage and causing the rest of the animals to panic. The noise level grew rapidly as dogs howled and banged against the bars of their cages; the rats all let out ear-splitting squeaks and shrieks, and even the rabbits, normally quiet and refined by comparison, stamped their feet and careered around their cages, turning over food pots and tossing hay and shavings on their way.

22

Betrayed

A loud knock on the office door made the three of them jump, their nerves raw and edgy by now.

"Come."

A short, round man waddled in. He had floppy grey hair, a neat moustache, walked with a stoop, and wore the outfit of a butler.

"Yes, Chamberlain?"

"You asked me to fetch mother, so she could be present at your negotiations with the foreign gentlemen, sir. She has arrived."

"Ah, good. Ask her to come in, will you? And I'd like you to be present too, if you don't mind."

"Not at all, sir."

Chamberlain left, returning a moment later with a small, dumpy, grey-haired old lady. Eric hardly knew her without the two plastic carriers usually tied to her coat. John's sharp intake of breath meant he had recognised her.

"So that's how he knew," he murmured.

The old lady made her way to Dr Sissington's desk, and took his hand. He relaxed visibly as she approached, and let her stroke his hand tenderly.

"Good to see you again after so long, sir," she said, her voice motherly and soft, "it's been far too long and I'm glad to be out of that place, with all those oddball people. Such bad habits. You could tell at a glance that they were not brought up properly. And there is a bit of a kerfuffle going on out there, dear boy. Some men with placards have taken control of your computer terminals, and your research scientists are being escorted from the premises. It doesn't look good I'm afraid. But let's get you sorted first, eh? You must let me massage your brow, like I used to when you were a child. That always helped make things better."

Eric moved for the first time since the old lady had walked in.

"Winnie?"

She turned to face him.

"Hello, boy. Yes, it's me, free of that smelly, filthy disguise at last. Live and learn, boy—some people will do anything for the ones they love. And as for me? I endured months of vermin, rotten food and body odour, so that Master Edwin would know all about you, what you did, where you went, and who with. A good disguise, don't you agree?"

Sprockett did not have the lightning quick reactions of a slip fielder at a cricket match. His mug was against his lips as the row started, and he flung it down, spilling hot fluid down his trousers. He stood up and marched from cage to cage, banging the doors with his fist, bellowing, "What's up, you rabble? Belt up, you 'orrible critters, before I use me prodder!"

This would normally have done the trick. Sprockett had been issued with a small device that could stun an animal with an electric shock, rather like a cattle prod but smaller—a true cattle prod would have killed any of these creatures outright. Every one of the animals in that room had seen it, and they were all too aware of the pain it inflicted. Normally, Sprockett only had to wave it around to get the cages to hush and the beasts to calm down. But not this time.

His attempts to shut them up had the opposite effect. By the time Sprockett had reached the door through which Thickpea had entered, the noise had risen to a deafening cacophony. And it worked. Under the cover of this amazing distraction, Thickpea had galloped across the room, leapt onto the work surface where Sprockett's mug lay on its side, then up again to the shelf that held the control box. With a huge effort, she launched herself at the red button, and fell against it with her whole weight. With a whirr followed by a clang, a massive bolt shot sideways, and every cage was open. A piercing alarm rang out, but it was almost drowned by the animal racket and made no difference to every single creature's bid for freedom.

Eric was speechless. He had trusted Winnie, almost as a mother. He had shared food with her, even snuggled down to sleep on a park bench with her, and here she was, spying for his own uncle. John had been right when he told him there was more to this matter than he knew, and when he said not to trust anybody. Eric sank back into his seat, still trying to get his head round this latest bombshell. Winnie turned back to Dr. Sissington.

A sudden shout from the crowd on the street grabbed their attention. Dr Sissington dashed to the window, looking down on the sight below. The sound of triumphant yells told him that the protesters were charging into his building en masse. It was no delicate foray into new territory, but a furious onslaught, as the whole rabble rushed the revolving doors causing them to jam shut and half a dozen of the vanguard protesters were squashed against the glass by the weight of the rest of them. This paused the invasion, but it was not long before a tall, bearded old man pushed to the front of the heap of yelping bodies and started to heave them out of the way, clearing a path for them to get into Sissington Towers. Old Yar was a valiant campaigner when his blood was up.

As Eric watched, he saw Newton gesturing the rest of the protesters to follow, and he and a petite figure in a balaclava—Eric guessed it was probably Bonnet—pushed their way inside. The doctor's face betrayed a hint of terror and he ran for the office door. As he reached it, whoops of glee and victory could be heard from the lobby, as the motley bunch of animal lovers shoved open the outer door of the laboratory, breaking through the expensive security lock. In came Old Yar, Newton and the almost unrecognisable Bonnet. Eric heard a rough, gravelly voice mutter, "Thanks, Libby," as the rest of the crowd poured in. Once in the lobby, they paused, wondering which door they needed to make for next.

John Bagnall was worried. This was not exactly what he'd had in mind. The force and enthusiasm of this victorious swarm threatened to wipe out any chance of acquiring solid evidence for his case if he was not careful. He marched purposefully to the office door, beckoned Old Yar and Bonnet inside, then pulled the doctor roughly by the arm to stop him leaving. This probably did him a favour; had the rabble got their hands on the doctor, there is no telling what they might have done to him.

He found Newton in the mob, and went over to him.

"Don't let anybody any further, okay? It won't be easy, but I don't want anything destroyed."

Newton nodded. He turned to face the rest, who were still swarming around aimlessly, unsure of what to do next.

"Come on," Newton's distinctively gruff tones bellowed over their uncertain murmurs, "we need to secure the building. The great Doctor Sissington can wait. Our first phase is complete. Now let's make sure we don't lose any of the others who have caused pain and death to animals. Agreed?"

A shout of approval went up as the majority of the crowd turned and left the lobby, heading back down to the large reception hall where they would plan a floor-by-floor sweep to check up on every company, and to make sure no laboratory workers had tried to hide in the other offices.

John closed and locked the office door. He needed to complete his mission without further interference. Winnie waited until the door was shut, then continued as if nothing unusual had happened. From the other side of the door, the sounds of footsteps, with accompanying cries of "Freedom for fur!" dwindled away as the lobby cleared.

"Now, tell me," Winnie said, sitting in her chair, straight backed and with her hands folded neatly on her lap, "where's Audrey? It's unlike my daughter to be late for an appointment."

Her voice was quite different now, the slightly posh accent replacing the London drawl she had affected while living at Hackney Mansions.

The doctor answered, deliberately calm and controlled in his manner.

"She's in custody—arrested at the hospital, but not until after she had succeeded."

Winnie stared at him, her eyes wide.

"But how? There was no reason for her to be suspected. A nurse in a hospital, that's hardly a sight to cause panic."

"She met—*him*," Chamberlain pointed accusingly at Eric. "He was there. The noise he made meant the crash team was called. Audrey lost her cool, I'm afraid—started saying too much, trying to blame the boy, said too much. Sorry, Mother."

"Is that all you have to say about your own sister's arrest?"

Another satisfied sigh escaped from John.

"Sister? Another relative, eh?" he mumbled to himself. It all made sense now. Doctor Sissington's manservant and housekeeper were brother and sister, and their mother, Winnie, had been—

"You were his nanny," Eric said slowly as the facts sank into place. "You cared for my uncle when he was a child. You've always been there, watching my family, hoping one day to inherit what isn't rightfully yours—"

"Not rightfully mine? Not rightfully mine?" Winnie bristled with anger. "How dare you, boy? What gives you the right to inherit anything from this man, a genius, who could save mankind from a host of terrible illnesses, and who happens to want a little something for himself and those who have nurtured him and his dreams in return?" She stalked round the office, pacing from wall to wall with determined precision. "Does that not make more sense, more logical than giving all his assets to some selfish youth who happens to be his only living relative? Oh, I'm sure the law will see it differently, but that doesn't make it right."

Bonnet moved slightly.

"But no law will support you," she almost whispered, as if scared to take part in the proceedings. "You seem to have forgotten the condition of the Sissington inheritance, Winnie. Nobody with a criminal record can benefit from the family riches."

Winnie's face seized up, tight in a grimace. She sat quite still, then through gritted teeth, said, "My dear girl, what can you mean?"

"It was your grandson that kidnapped me. We called him Blondie, remember? That young man with almost white hair, and your nose and other facial features. I notice things like that. I am rather interested in characters, you may not have noticed. And he talked about you when I was in the house."

"What? How can you say that? It can't be true."

"He gave you away, Winnie, or whatever your name is. He talked to his dad on the phone, about your—asteroids."

Winnie looked puzzled, but John nodded vigorously.

"Bonnet, you've done it! Well done!"

Bonnet sat staring at her hands, talking in a hushed tone but everybody was listening avidly.

"We were doing the washing at the hostel yesterday. The laundry was packed with people bringing down piles of clothes, blankets, anything they owned that could be shoved in a washing machine. My hats were on the spin cycle, and I was waiting for them when Winnie came down with her two carrier bags of stuff. The helper, Rachel, a lovely lass with a Liverpool accent I must try to copy one day, offered to change Winnie's two bags for new ones, but she refused, saying—she didn't know where they had been, she might catch all sorts of anthracites. It's well known, her mixing up medical words, but I didn't make the connection with Blondie—"

"His name is Carl!" Winnie snarled.

"If you say so," Bonnet responded, "or Kal, as he preferred to be known."

Kal? Something heavy nudged Eric's brain as another fact dropped into place.

"Kal," Bonnet continued, "is the boy who rules the Fractured Jaw Gang on the streets near Seven Sisters, remember? We never see him without his hoodie, pulled over his hair to cover it completely, so we would never recognise him when he was on the streets, looking for Eric, running errands between his mother in hiding as a bag lady and his dad, still working for Dr Sissington. He was the one to pass on the news, and take instructions. Only he insulted—that—man—Sprockett—once too often, and the oaf flipped. Chucked him out of the window. End of Carl, as far as this adventure's concerned."

Sprocket stood rooted to the spot, the floor suddenly covered with dozens of small, furry blurs running hither and thither, trying to find an escape route. Rabbits, rats, tiny marmosets, mice, puppies and larger capuchin monkeys, all shot across the room, each one desperate for freedom and galvanised into furious action, even if they did not know exactly what they were doing or where they should go. All that animal energy, pent up and controlled in their cages for so long, overflowed, causing them to gallop round searching for somewhere safe.

The smaller the creature, the more of a blur it made as it hared around. A white mouse jumped up to the top of its cage, pausing to look around, then dived into a large barrel of food left open on the floor. A russet-coloured marmoset, following its breed's instinctive defences, climbed upwards, shinning up the side of a shelving unit and leaping effortlessly to the air conditioning unit in the ceiling. There it hung, looking down at the mayhem below, seeming to scream encouragement to the others. Puppies that had never been allowed out of their cages in their short lives were terrified, whimpering pitifully, wee-ing and poo-ing all over the floor, and heading for any other warm, furry thing within in the hope of finding comfort. The rats headed straight for the floor, zooming behind benches and taking the occasional nibble out of anything they found lying around. One such rat took a chunk out of an electric cable; with a loud fizzing noise, it died instantly, and all the lights went out. In the dark, the noise was deafening. Even the rabbits, normally quiet, sedate animals, were squeaking with terror. A thick, moving carpet of fur made its way to the only light in the room, which came through the open door where Sprockett stood, paralysed by the sight. He would lose his job over this. That was the only thought that filled his clogged brain.

Then one monkey, a capuchin, jumped onto the stool, stood on its hind legs and held out its forelegs. It was a clear call for silence, although it took a few moments for all the creatures to see it. The room fell quiet. Every pair of eyes was turned to the capuchin, who issued a series of low grunts which slowly grew in volume and built to loud shrieks, and clearly pointed at Sprockett. It was a call for action, for revenge, for an attack.

Winnie's face looked like thunder. Eric had not thought it possible for so much hate to appear on one face. She spat as she spoke now, the rage barely controlled.

"All those months in such filth, I could not have stood it much longer! Having to use all that modern speak, with its dreadful grammar and lack of correctness—so unlike me, as they would have me say. And the company I had to keep—hardly suitable for a lady of my standing. That old sea dog, with his unbelievable lies about life on the oceans—what twaddle!"

Old Yar had stood in silence, not sure what was occurring; but he bridled at this barb and muttered something under his breath about sea serpents, harpoons, and plenty of vinegar. Winnie continued to rant.

"Then *her*—this young daft girl there, with her precious hats! Needs to see a doctor, in my opinion. And as for the boy—how stupid can you get, running from a crash just because he thought he caused it. Ha! Who'd have thought he was so arrogant as to think it was all because of him? Mind you, his foul temper proved very useful. It was easy to blame the crash on a selfish young lout who wasn't getting everything he wanted."

Winnie paused, looking into the faces of those staring dumbly at her. She was enjoying being the centre of attention.

"Master Edwin knew that inheriting the small legacy that belonged to his sister, your mother, would give him just enough money to begin his plans, and it was the easiest thing of all to get Carl to fiddle with the brakes on the car, so that—BANG!"

She said it in such a light tone of voice that is was more like telling a joke. It left Eric, John, Old Yar and Bonnet cold inside. Winnie calmed, sat back in her chair and looked at Bonnet.

"And as for *you*, you are clearly your mother's daughter. Always meddling, that Doldrum, never able to leave well alone. I should have got rid of you just like I did with her."

All eyes in the room turned to Bonnet. The lass sat stock-still, her gaze fixed on a patch of carpet by her feet. A deep breath erupted from the depths of her thin frame.

"You killed my mother?" She spoke slowly and precisely, every word carefully enunciated. "The kindest, most gentle person I have known, who brought me up in a clean, safe home until we were forced to leave, thrown into the streets by a ruthless landlord. But did she give up? Did she succumb to despair, degradation, dirt? No! She found a safe harbour, moving us into Hackney Mansions with Old Yar, and kept us fed and warm. And that huge Jamaican grin that invigorated us! And—" she turned to Old Yar, who sat in stunned silence by her side, "do you remember that laugh?"

The old sailor nodded slowly. Bonnet grinned, despite her misery. It was a wide, warm, welcoming smile that touched every—nearly every—person in the room.

"She could break ice with the warmth of her laugh. I've seen the coldest souls thaw in my mum's presence. And you killed her." She swivelled round to stare at Winnie. "Just to be in her place, near Eric? Was that the reason? To keep an eye on him, befriend him, eventually to get him out of your way? You destroyed a life, for what? Money? Was that it?"

A stunned silence followed this outburst. Eric remembered how he had mentioned to Thickpea that everything would be solved by Sherlock Bonnet. How right he had been—but at such a cost; Bonnet learning that her mother had died at the hands of this witch. A twinge of guilt passed through him as he thought of Thickpea for the first time in what felt like ages. Where was she? What was happening out there? Was she in danger, with such a mass of people loose in the building?

Beneath the mountain of fur, teeth and claws, lay Sprockett. Hundreds of tiny lifetimes' worth of hatred and fear were released in this organised, focussed attack. Every creature had a score to settle, and in a matter of minutes, the cause of so much pain and unhappiness was paying for his cruelty.

The mice ran all over him, taking nips whenever bare flesh showed. Rabbit claws can cause deep, painful grooves when used in anger, and before long Sprockett's face was scarred with deep, red lines. The monkeys ripped his clothing, pulling at his fingers and ears, gnawing his fingernails and shoelaces. One puppy, confused and afraid, was half licking, half eating the man's socks. But it was the rats that headed for the more delicate bits of Sprockett's anatomy. Within moments of their arrival, he was yelping with agony and begging for mercy. Apart from the other bits of him that proved to be gourmet rat food, the rats made sure that Horace Sprockett would never see again.

Rolling on the floor, crying for it to stop, the victim heard a gasp of horror as reinforcements arrived for Sprockett. Every animal abandoned the attack and ran for their lives. Strong hands carefully tended the bloody mess that had been Sprockett, yelling urgently for an ambulance to be summoned.

As for the newly freed lab animals, a new life beckoned. Some of them decided to stay, and made homes in some comfortable corner of Sissington Towers. Many of them made straight for the stairs, scurrying across the foyer and leaving the building—but most of them did not survive once outside. One particular dark rat, the one who had started the rumpus when he saw Thickpea coming to help them, made a beeline for a cosy home that happened to be heading back to Hackney Mansions when the day was over. Whether he had picked up some message from Thickpea was never discovered; but Bonnet's bag proved to be a perfect temporary home for one newly freed creature.

Of the men who entered the animal room, not a soul noticed a tiny, inert body lying beside the mug, just above the gibbering blob on the floor that was Horace Sprockett. A rat lay there, hardly breathing, her heartbeat no more that the slightest brush of a feather. Thickpea was in trouble.

23

The Blue Bottle

The silence was broken by a loud, shrill scream. It came from a distance, and Doctor Sissington sat upright, his eyes towards the door.

"That came from the lab," he remarked, and nodded to Chamberlain. Without a word, the manservant left the room at a run, the screech getting louder as the door opened, then dulling a little as it closed after him. Nobody spoke. The hush was not disturbed until, a few moments later, Chamberlain came back. He was out of breath and, as he entered, he leaned against the door as if keeping out some terrible force.

"Oh, dear heaven," he moaned, his eyes wild with fear, "I can't believe it, what a dreadful sight, I think I'm going to—"

And without warning, he lurched into a corner and threw up on the floor. Still nobody moved.

As he regained a little composure, Chamberlain came back to stand in front of his master.

"My apologies, sir, it was the shock. What I saw ... in the lab," he started, then retched again. It took several attempts before he could speak properly.

"It was Sprockett ... must have gone through there to reach the far doors to lock them securely ... the rats, and the others, you know? ... they were out of their cages ... they were climbing all over him ... no, don't ask me to describe ... it was ... The man was lying in a heap, in a corner, his clothes torn, his face scratched and bitten ... blood everywhere ... he was covering his face with his hands, daubed with blood ... but his mind, sir ... he was squealing, like a frightened animal. His mind has gone. He's nothing but a massive hunk of gristle and skin, with a whimpering, tortured creature inside. Those—rats! It was the rats that have done for him, sir!"

Winnie clutched her chest, gasping for breath. Chamberlain crumpled in a heap on the floor and the doctor stared straight ahead, his glassy eyes not focussing on anything. A nasty little demon inside Eric whispered, 'Serve him right, to get him back for all the pain he had inflicted on the rats when he reigned supreme in the lab, making them suffer in so many horrible ways.' He was sure that Thickpea had had a part in this. It was her revenge for the pain that ogre had made her and her kind suffer. But Eric was not sure what sort of life Horace Sprockett would have from now on.

The doctor looked at Eric.

"Well, boy," he lifted himself upright in his chair, "now you know. You are my only living relative, the one who will inherit all my worldly goods, the one who will take on responsibility for all you see around you. I can't say I'm pleased at the thought. There are people I would rather have passed my wealth and my laboratory to, but—" he cast his eye around the room, "—I suppose it's not the thing to admit to in such illustrious company!"

Eric did not move, but his insides were burning with anger. He was clearly being provoked, and he would not give his uncle the satisfaction of making him react. Doctor Sissington continued.

"I despised your parents. They had nothing to do with my success. They never showed the gritty determination needed to get where I am now. Too soft, that was their trouble. And you are just the same, boy. Nothing but a big, soppy coward. Running from the crash, ducking your responsibilities, hiding with these—lowlifes. Hardly a Sissington, are you?"

Eric stood slowly, and moved towards his uncle.

"If I have to be like you to win, then I would rather lose. You are the reason for all the misery I have suffered. You are the cause of so much suffering in this lab. You are the one who led Winnie and her family to act as they have. Grief, pain, death—quite a collection you've made. Well, I think you ought to know, you can't hurt me anymore. You've done everything you can to destroy me—and I'm still here! I call that failure, don't you?"

A murmur of approval came from Old Yar. John Bagnall looked grave, but he nodded in agreement. Bonnet, tears dripping down her cheeks, merely swallowed and blew her nose. Doctor Sissington sagged in his chair. It was the first sign of defeat he had shown, but there was still a gleam of madness in his eyes.

"So, you think I am finished? Not quite, my boy. Not quite."

He toyed with several small objects on the desk in front on him.

"No more loose ends. I can't abide loose ends. Nanny taught me that. Keep things tidy and it will all turn out right in the end, she always said. Well, I think that about covers everything," he reached down to open a drawer. "And I can see that the outcome is not going to be quite as I planned, but—"

With a sudden movement he picked up a small blue bottle, and in a single movement he pulled a cork from the top of the bottle, tipped it up to his mouth and swallowed the contents in one gulp. There was no time for anybody to stop him, but when she saw what he had done, Winnie cried out in anguish.

"Master Edwin, what was that? Is it—no! Oh my dear, what have you done?"

The doctor laughed, a hollow sound that echoed in his chest, and ended in a gurgle as a breath caught in his throat.

John and Chamberlain ran to the table, reaching it together, one on each side of the doctor. John retrieved the bottle from his grasp and read the label.

"Emotion concentrate. Use with caution."

He sat slumped in his chair, a half smile on his lips, as he looked up at them both in turn.

"Time for the last experiment, eh? Let's see if this magical potion will cure me, shall we?"

The room was heavy with silence. The man behind the desk was grinning, quite absorbed in himself and unaware of the small crowd of people standing in dumb horror as they watched him. They saw him suddenly sit upright, his back regimental and his eyes glazed, then slowly he sink back into his chair, as though he was melting. The grin remained, fixed and rigid, and he spoke between gritted teeth.

"Oh yes, I can definitely feel something happening. It's as though I'm floating through something syrupy and sticky, a slow drift from cloud to cloud, with tiny beads of water trickling down the back of my neck—"

He reached up, rubbing his neck as though trying to remove a fly.

"Mmmm, most odd, now it's feeling hot. No, more than hot—I think I'm beginning to roast—oh, that's not nice, not nice at all. I don't like this—"

He wriggled in his chair, as though Old Yar had shoved his old pet ferret down his trousers. His agitation was growing as the sensations he experienced were becoming more and more uncomfortable and painful.

"No! Stop it! It never seemed to hurt the test subjects like this—why me? And—oh, I can feel—somebody in this room is feeling—terror! I can read it! And—another of you—what's that, a cruel delight at my pain? Is that what I can see? And there's more—so much more—"

As the empathy scanner took hold, Dr Sissington's eyes grew huge and round. His mouth fell open, his body stiff and strangely contorted, as he froze in position. He looked as if he were trying to scratch his back with one hand while pulling up one of his socks with the other, his head twisted sideways and facing upwards in a grotesque manner.

There was nothing anybody could do. Everybody was on his or her feet, their eyes glued to Dr. Sissington's face, watching for changes, improvements, miracles. They were all witnessing the final stage of the grand scheme, the conclusion of Doctor Edwin Sissington's master plan. He would never be given the chance to complete his work otherwise. This was the only way he would ever discover the truth, if his wonder drug would cure him of the disease that was killing him cell by cell, agonisingly.

Nothing happened for several minutes. The room was full of silence, again. Then, without warning, the doctor crumpled onto the floor, flowing off the chair like a liquid. His face was grey, and Winnie was the first to reach him. She knelt beside her charge and stroked his hair—only to find it coming off in her fingers by the handful.

"Aaah! No, not his lovely hair, not his hair!"

The strands of hair stuck in her nails as she pulled away from him, aghast at what she had done. Dr. Sissington lifted his hand to his face, and a groan issued from his mouth as he rolled from side to side. It sounded as though he was in pain, but he did not say any recognisable word. Then his hands fell to his sides, palms upmost. Eric stared, along with the rest, to see that the skin on his face and hands had wrinkled to the texture of a prune. Deep, dark bags clung to the bottom of his eye sockets. The skin was blotchy and veined. The man had aged instantaneously. Whatever cocktail of drugs he had drunk from the blue bottle, it had brought on a reaction so violent that his body could not cope. It was giving up, with a ferocious speed.

At the end, when he was unable to shrivel any more, Doctor Sissington suffered an agony he had never dreamed of. In his last moments, as life ebbed away, he felt what Thickpea had been able to feel, only on a dreadful, magnified scale. The huge dose of empathy scanner he had taken opened the doorway to every emotion in that room, each one swollen as if through a giant telescope, all on top of one other, mingled, knotted, fighting, swelling and ultimately suffocating his ability to think. The overpowering, overwhelming sensations, one on top of another, confused, crushed and ultimately overloaded his mind.

Doctor Sissington died, quite insane.

In the animal room, a slim flicker of life remained in Thickpea's valiant heart. She knew she was dying, but she also knew she had done everything in her limited power to save the lives of the other animals who had been kept in that building of torture. As her eyes closed for the last time, she felt a slow, warm glow creep along her veins. A contented, loving glow filled her, and a long, low sigh escaped from her tiny mouth. The final thoughts were for Eric, the boy who had taken her from her wild existence and who had made it possible for her to experience such joy and fulfilment. Then, silently, peacefully, Thickpea's courageous spirit departed her fragile body, her work done, the world a better place for her having been in it.

Winnie screamed, and leapt away from the twisted corpse. The rest were paralysed by the appalling sight. John was the first in the room to regain his composure. He flew to the door, turned the key and opened it wide, screaming for an ambulance. Immediately, three austere-looking men with large briefcases and bowler hats were marching in.

"In here!" John shouted, and they were joined by Libby, the receptionist, who had shown the invading protesters which way to go—her last act as Special Branch informer under John Bagnall—and a handful of the white-coated lab technicians who had never been allowed into the boss's office before. Chamberlain was now comforting his mother, who wept uncontrollably in her chair. Eric, Old Yar and Bonnet still sat against the wall, watching the scene as if not part of it. One of the MI5 men led Winnie and Chamberlain out to a car and drove them away quietly and efficiently. Eric never saw either of them again.

He was quite alone now. His father was dead, murdered by that witch of a nurse. Now his uncle had killed himself in a manner more gruesome than even he realised. Eric had lived without them both for the past four years, but his future would be shaped by their deaths. Now that he had returned to the real world, the boy knew he must tie up the loose ends, then think about his prospects. The muddle in his head that was called a brain would find itself unknotted again, but not until every-thing was sorted. Not least was his concerns about where he would find a home, should he decide not to return to the streets. And to be honest, that was no longer an option. He had moved on from that world.

Old Yar was sitting alone on his office chair, muttering to himself about awful deaths he had seen in his long lifetime, but how this scientist boffin's demise had been the worst, apart from the young fella-me-lad he'd watched being slowly devoured by a giant conger eel the size of the Blackwall Tunnel. There was nobody listening to him.

Conclusion

John and the Special Branch officers then covered Doctor Sissington's body with a coat they had found on a fancy coat rack in the office, and began systematically to search the room. Eric took the opportunity to leave and went on a search of his own—for Thickpea.

He followed the sounds coming from the left-hand doorway. Coos and murmurs of "Oooh, it's sooo cute!" and "Look at that, it's eating out of my hand!" were coming from a handful of people, each one crouching and stroking one of the animals set free by Thickpea. This was not the animal room in which Sprockett still squealed and mumbled to himself in a corner, waiting for the ambulance that would take him away to be cared for; no, this was a room with broad work surfaces, each one stocked with test tubes, microscopes and a host of technological wizardry designed to help the scientists who had worked there in their quest for a medical miracle. The rats, bunnies, monkeys and pooches, having done their work on Sprockett, had left that room without delay, eager to leave all traces of their past behind.

Eric walked towards the door of the animal room, afraid of what he would see in there. He remembered what Chamberlain had said about Sprockett—not a pretty sight. But he knew he had no choice. He must find Thickpea. Pushing the door ajar, he peeked round it.

"Thickpea?"

Eric called tentatively, but there was no response. He felt a gentle nuzzle against his foot, and, looking down, saw a beautiful black and white rabbit jumping up at his leg.

It stared straight at him, then hopped into the room, checking over its shoulder to make sure the boy was following. Eric walked behind it, passed the rows of empty cages, closer with each step to the snivelling Sprockett. But the bear of a man paid no attention to Eric. He was in a world of his own hugging himself and squealing, his nose twitching, his feet tapping a strange rhythm on the floor. He was not a threat any longer.

The rabbit led Eric to a tiny, still ball of fur at the far end on the room. It lay on the floor, almost invisible in the shadows. Very gingerly he picked up the body of his beloved rat, and walked back out of the room.

His fingers were wrapped round the small furry bundle, but there was no sign of life. It was quite, quite cold. She looked as if she was simply asleep. It was hard for Eric to believe she wouldn't ever wake up. Her body looked old, her skin flabby and her teeth loose, and some of her hair came off in Eric's fingernails. Then, as he felt the soft fur against his fingers, Eric noticed something shiny between the rat's front paws. Very carefully he prised them apart, and found a miniature gold football boot. Thickpea had held on to the charm he had found in the house where Sprockett had chucked Carl out of the window, keeping it close to her body in the pocket, then, when her life had finished, she clutched it to her fur for comfort. She knew it had belonged to Eric, and in the last minutes it gave her extra strength. The shock of the number and strength of emotions the rat had experienced that day had proved too much for her rapidly ageing body, causing her tiny organs to fail. Eric gulped back the tears. Yet another minor tremor he had suffered today. He wasn't sure he could take much more.

There is no need to dwell on what happened in the following days. It was a very lonely, painful time for Eric, and he spent much of the time alone, deep in thought. There were many decisions to be made, but one thing he was sure of was that the vagrant life and all the characters and places that it had included, would be part of his future. He was indeed the sole heir to the Sissington money, but after the court cases, the allegations of treason against his uncle, and the closing of the lab and the compensation claims that followed, there wasn't very much left. Eric was not bothered by that. He had learned enough about life to know there are more important things than money. And anyway, four years on the streets had given him a wealth of knowledge that would see him into an uncertain future, some of it very useful. That, and his new friendship with John Bagnall, could make for a very interesting future. Time would tell.

He let his wanderings carry him past the makeshift homes he had used over the past four years, and a few days later, Eric returned with Bonnet to Hackney Mansions. Old Yar was seated in his comfy chair in the old staffroom, his face set in a granite pose of defiance and sadness. It had taken no time at all for the news of the incident at the laboratory to reach the hostel, and as the Christmas season passed and the dozens of homeless people left for their own patches, the story spread with them. Everybody knew of the boy who had been found out, who had regained his home, but at a terrible cost. The old seaman pushed his way out of his chair with an effort, waddled in his rolling stride towards them, and gave Eric and Bonnet rib-crushing hugs of love and support.

"Well, my powder monkey," he mumbled through his whisky-smelling beard, "you have a new life now. And so do we, without you. And we have a new recruit here, see? I don't think you've met—"

There, sitting in another old armchair with broken springs and faded covers, was Newton, the crippled man with the scar on his face. He raised a hand in greeting.

The four of them sat and talked for hours, discussing the whole affair, looking at how things might have turned out differently. After a while, Eric went out into the old playground, dug a deep hole in the flowerbed and buried Thickpea along with all his precious possessions he had salvaged from the three havens. He wouldn't need them now, not where he was going to live.

As he put the last spade-load of soil on the grave, he heard a tiny noise behind him. There, watching him round the edge of the building, was a rat. Larger and darker than Thickpea had been, but holding its head up in just the same manner, as if sniffing out its prey. The creature snuffled, then squeaked, and washed its face with its paws, quite unconcerned that Eric had invaded its space. Then, as he watched, Eric noticed a subtle, unexpected movement. The rat was shuddering as it watched him. It was not particularly cold that day, the threat of snow and ice having passed with the festive season. The rat had felt something else, something deeper, something that could not be seen. It had sensed the boy's pain.

Very gently Eric made his way indoors and headed straight upstairs to one of the old classrooms where he remembered seeing an old cardboard shoebox. Then he would have to scrounge some cheese, and remind himself how to catch a rat …

978-0-595-46620-7
0-595-46620-6

Printed in the United Kingdom
by Lightning Source UK Ltd.
126948UK00001B/61-69/A